Other books by Betty Thomason Owens

The Legacy Series

Amelia's Legacy
Carlotta's Legacy
Rebecca's Legacy

The Kinsman Redeemer Series

Annabelle's Ruth
Sutter's Landing
Annabelle's Joy

STILL WATER
a Home Found Suspense
BETTY THOMASON OWENS

P

Write Integrity Press

Still Water
© 2021 Betty Thomason Owens
ISBN: 978-1-944120-98-6

This book is a work of fiction. Names, characters, places, and incidents are either products of the author's imagination or used fictitiously. Any similarity to actual people and/or events is purely coincidental.

All quoted Scripture passages are taken from the KING JAMES VERSION (KJV): KING JAMES VERSION, public domain.

Published by

Pursued Books, an imprint of
Write Integrity Press, LLC
PO Box 702852
Dallas, TX 75370

Find out more about the author, Betty Thomason Owens, at her website: BettyThomasonOwens.com
or on her author page at WriteIntegrity.com

Printed in the United States of America.

In Loving Memory of

Nike Navor Chillemi

Contents

CHAPTER ONE

April 12, 1971
Asheville, North Carolina
Lisa Oliver

*M*y *father was dead?*

The antiseptic smell of the consultation room threatened to expunge the crackers I had recently eaten.

Doctor Rutledge laid a gentle hand on my arm. "I'm sorry, Miss Oliver. Your father died at the scene of the accident."

The air left my lungs. Tears burned my eyes. This couldn't be happening.

A nurse rubbed my back but said nothing.

I managed to croak out, "Mom?"

Dr. Rutledge shook his head. "She survived the

accident and the trip to the hospital. We did everything we could, but her injuries were too severe."

I shook my head. "No."

Surely, I had misunderstood. God would not let this happen to me. Would He?

I stared at my trembling hands. Maybe they should check my pulse. One moment, my heart was racing. The next, it ceased beating. I looked from the doctor to the silent nurse and back again. "What happened? My dad was a great driver."

Neither answered for a moment, but then the nurse sitting beside me spoke up. "As far as we know, it was just an accident. Treacherous mountain road on a rainy night."

I pressed my palms to the base of my throat and rocked forward and back, but it brought me no comfort. "Dad drove semis for a living." The nurse's gaze held mine as I pressed my point. "He was used to inclement weather and bad road conditions. He sought out less-traveled ways and always preferred to drive at night."

Dr. Rutledge shook his head again. "Sometimes there's no reasonable explanation for why things happen, Miss Oliver."

"This can't be happening." The pain poured out of me with a sob. I couldn't even put into words the rest of my questions.

"Perhaps you'd like to be alone for a few moments?" The doctor stood and stepped to the door. After giving my arm a final pat, the nurse followed him from the room.

Once I was alone, the tears overwhelmed me. I jumped up, paced to the window and back in repetitive motion.

Tired of pacing, I sat in the chair. I had emptied a full box of tissues before the door opened again. I expected to see Dr. Rutledge or the nurse, but it was neither.

"Lisa Oliver?" A tall, willowy man entered. He had dark hair, graying at the temples. He was dressed in a suit, though it was well past midnight.

I nodded and breathed in and out, trying to gain control. Then I noticed the Bible in his hand. A preacher?

"Miss Oliver, I'm James Tobey, the hospital's chaplain. Dr. Rutledge asked me to check on you." He sat beside me in one of the blue chairs. "I'm so, so sorry for your loss. Can I get you anything?"

I shook my head. "No, thank you." Tears pooled. Surely, I'd cried enough by now.

The lines of his forehead deepened as his eyes held mine. "In a few minutes, we'll go to another room. I'm afraid it's necessary for you, as next of kin, to identify your parents."

I bit my lip to stop the trembling. Of course, I'd have to do that. Part of me wanted to see them. And part of me wanted to run away. My heart raced again, and my breath came in short spurts.

The door opened. This time, an orderly beckoned.

Mr. Tobey stood and waited for me to rise.

I dabbed my nose with an overused tissue, picked up my purse and tucked it under my arm. Maybe they would have more tissues where we were going.

The long, dimly lit corridor echoed with our footsteps as we followed the orderly. Near the end, he opened a door.

With a hand at my mid-back, Mr. Tobey ushered me inside.

I had no idea what to expect. Would they be battered, bruised, bloody? My head swam, so I welcomed Mr. Tobey's supporting arm.

Surreal. That's the only word I could summon. Maybe I was in shock, but my parents' faces didn't affect me as I expected. I nodded but couldn't speak.

"Do you need a moment?" Mr. Tobey asked.

I shook my head. "No." *They're not here*, I wanted to say. Those were their bodies, but they were empty shells.

They'd gone again, moved on to another place. But this time, I couldn't follow.

I stumbled as Mr. Tobey led me back to the private waiting area. He opened the door. "Sit in here. I'll be right back."

Maybe I had a choice, but at that moment, I couldn't come up with anything else to do. I couldn't leave, not while Mom and Dad's remains lay down the hall. Maybe I should have stayed with them.

I sat in the same chair and waited for someone to tell me what to do next.

Mr. Tobey returned with two paper cups that hopefully held coffee, a small bag, and a couple napkins. He set one of the cups on the table beside me and then sat in an adjacent chair. "I got us Danishes. They're fresh." He held the bag for me.

I wasn't sure I could eat, though I probably should've been hungry. It had been almost twenty-four hours since I'd had anything. I took the pastry and a napkin and leaned back in the chair.

Mr. Tobey pulled packets of sugar and powdered cream from his jacket pocket and placed them on the table. "I didn't know how you liked your coffee." He emptied a couple packets of cream into his and stirred with a plastic stir-stick.

Creamy. That's how I liked my coffee. I emptied the remaining four packets of creamer into the cup. After a bite of the delicious Danish and a few sips of hot coffee, my brain began to function again. An odd sort of peace settled over me. I looked at Mr. Tobey. "What happens next?" I tore another piece off the diminishing Danish.

"There's paperwork coming. Probably a lot of it. They'll need to know what to do with ..." he nodded toward the hall door. "Your parents' bodies."

Panic crept back in. *How should I know what to do?* "Is there someone who can help me make that decision?"

He nodded. "I can refer you to someone. He's a funeral director. He can help you decide what's best, whether you want to transport them back home, or—" he stopped speaking when I shook my head.

"There's no need for that. We have no family. My parents were, um, they didn't have a lot of friends. We moved a lot." I put the final piece of the pastry into my mouth, wishing for a few more bites.

He nodded, as though he understood. "Was your dad in the service?"

"No, he just couldn't be still." I attempted a smile.

A knock at the door preceded another nurse. She

looked fresh, as though she'd just come on shift. "We're ready, Jim."

He stood, coffee in hand. "You can bring your coffee."

I hung my purse over my shoulder and picked up my cup before joining the nurse at the door.

She smiled. "I'm Beverly, Miss Oliver. I'm so sorry for your tragic loss. We're going to my office where you'll sign some forms, and then we'll let you go get some rest."

I nodded as a new thought came to mind. "Will I have to pay?" Because really, I had no money. "Dad didn't carry medical insurance. He didn't like it."

She nodded. "It's kind of a necessary evil these days. But no, you won't need to pay. Your father did have car insurance. They found the card in his glove compartment. We've already called the company. I don't think you'll have to worry about anything."

Almost an hour later, Beverly escorted me to the main waiting room where Mr. Tobey stood in conversation with a pleasant-looking middle-aged woman.

"God bless you, Lisa." Beverly gave my hand a firm squeeze. "Jim will take good care of you now."

Jim Tobey smiled. "Thank you, Beverly. Miss Oliver, this is my wife, Thea. I asked her to join us. We'd like you to come to our home where you can get some rest."

I looked from one to the other, not really liking the idea, but what choice did I have? At least they seemed nice.

On the way out the door, we were met by the orderly who'd taken me to view my parents. He handed me a small, plastic bag containing Mom's purse and Dad's wallet, along with a few other personal items. I hugged the bag to my chest, staring straight ahead.

This had to be a nightmare.

CHAPTER TWO

April 12, 1971
Asheville, North Carolina
Jake Bradley

I'd been standing at the front desk in the police station when the call came in. Overnight, there'd been a fatal accident on U.S. Route 25, a dangerous stretch of road in good weather. Last night's had been turbulent.

On a whim, I left the precinct office and drove toward the site of the accident. My job as a crime reporter for the *Asheville Summary* spurred me into action. Maybe this accident would give me a chance at something different, something beyond the muggings and robberies I normally covered. A human-interest piece to garner positive attention.

Was I ambulance chasing? Maybe, but it was worth it if I managed to come up with a story. There was something about this one.

I drove through downtown streets toward Route 25. The fatality aspect likely meant they had the site roped off and easy to find. If the cops were still investigating the scene, I'd have to use my ingenuity to get past them. I was flying solo here, without the benefit of an assignment.

Thanks to an elitist group of good-ole-boy coworkers, a newbie like me dared not step on anyone's toes. I'd already tried it a time or two and been chewed out by the chief—much to the pleasure of said coworkers.

A state trooper pulled away from the side of the road as I passed the location. I couldn't be sure if he was the only one there, so I drove a ways before turning around and then parked in a secluded spot about a quarter of a mile from the place where I'd seen the patrolman.

Before leaving the car, I put my work shoes in the floorboard, slipped on the hiking boots I always carried, clipped on my press badge, and grabbed a camera from the back seat.

Closer to the accident scene, the road's shoulder narrowed, dropping off sharply into a ravine. I heard the river before it came into view. A rocky stream on a good day, a raging rapid after a hard rain like the one last night.

After a quick survey that gave me a possible trajectory of the vehicle, I made my way carefully down the incline. The moisture content of the soil beneath my feet made progress slow.

Like a hunter, I walked flat-footed, making as little noise as possible. If anyone was still about, I didn't want to announce my presence. And if I stumbled on another reporter, I could get fired without a really good reason for being here. I wasn't too worried, though. I'd been told I had a great poker face. I'd always been able to bluff my way out of most anything.

A piece of a mirror sparkled on the ground. The top of a small tree lay beside it. To my right, up the steep grade, I could make out the path of the car, slamming against one mature tree, mowing down several little ones, and flattening the bushes as it came.

I crouched beside deep ruts and flattened briars where the vehicle must have landed. Roof-side down, is what I'd heard. Must've been a grisly scene. I snapped a couple of photos.

On high alert, I inched my way toward the riverbank, taking pictures as I moved nearer. Each time a car passed on the road, I stood still and waited. I didn't want to be caught trespassing. Even if I came up with a decent story to tell, I was taking a chance. The relationship between me and my editor was strained. I've tried not to care, but I'd prefer to leave this job on my own terms.

I looked around me. There was nothing here but the obvious aftermath of a collision between a vehicle and the ground. Bark missing from a nearby tree added to the narrative. I raised my camera and clicked. Had the occupants been thrown free of the wreckage?

I'd heard the driver died at the scene. His passenger survived a few hours longer. Had they left a family behind? I'd have to check that out.

I stepped onto an overhanging rock and eyed the stream. I noted where the waterline had been overnight, several feet above its current level. Had something washed downstream?

Behind me, car doors slammed. I sought a hiding place and found one upstream. I crouched by a washout beneath the roots of a giant oak tree.

After several minutes, two men dressed in plain clothes appeared. Detectives, or just curious like me? If they were detectives, I had nothing to fear, but something kept me rooted to the spot. I watched from my hiding place, hoping to garner information worthy of a story.

"It's been picked clean," the first man said.

"Maybe. Maybe not. Keep looking. We can't go back without it."

Huh. That didn't sound like something a detective would say, unless they'd lost something important. I strained my ears as the two made their way downstream. Could I follow without being detected?

The sound of their bickering reached me.

"You shouldn't have been following them so close."

"How'd I know he was going to lose it? He's a professional."

"Was a professional. Now he's just dead."

"Shut yer mouth. Sound carries near water."

The interesting conversation ceased as the men continued downstream. I crept out of my hiding place but stayed out of sight. I happened to locate a deer path through the ravine which allowed me to follow the voices at a distance. My country-boy upbringing came in handy.

Twenty minutes passed in silence as the men searched for whatever they had lost. When they headed back toward me, I ducked down into the thicket and waited, hoping for more conversation.

They stopped so close I held my breath. Had they seen me? Had the camera lens glinted in the sunlight? I was desperate for air when one of them finally spoke.

"We can't show up without it."

"No choice. We don't report in, boss will send the ankle-buster. You don't want that."

Ankle-buster?

As they moved away, I drew a deep breath but held my position until I heard car doors slam.

I'd have loved to get a picture of the two, but they would have heard the click of the camera. Like the guy said. Sound carried near water.

Questions swirled in my mind. Who were they, and what were they looking for?

When I dared leave my hiding place, I jogged back down to the embankment and picked my way through the weeds flattened by high water. I had no idea what I was looking for, but something niggled at my mind. I stopped, raised my camera, and adjusted the lens to focus on the far side of creek.

Nothing, which in itself was odd. No flotsam typical of post-flooding. The place was clean. Someone had already swept it. Who, and why?

I'd been at the site longer than intended, but when I finally crawled back up to the road, I drove until I found a phone booth in front of a convenience store a few miles past the crash site. I switched shoes and left my press pass in the car.

The receptionist at the office answered.

"Lucky Bishop, please." My friend would give me the lowdown on what I'd missed.

His voice was the next one I heard. "Where've you been, you sly dog? Weren't you supposed to turn in a story today? Hamilton is fuming. He keeps mumbling about three strikes."

Uh oh. "I was at the precinct this morning. Nothing much going on there, but I heard a couple of the cops talking about that fatality last night."

"You better not let the boss know you've been sniffing around that story, he assigned it to Tillman."

"Yeah, I figured. But there's something about it. I can't seem to let it go."

"Oh, so I guess you've been chasing down leads?" My friend actually chuckled as though it were a joke.

"Sort of."

"I taught you better than that, Jake. You can't horn in on another guy's story. You better get back here and try to save your job."

"I have one more stop to make, then I'll be in," I promised, though I wasn't sure it was true.

"You better make it quick. I don't know how much longer I can cover for you."

"I appreciate it." I hung up the phone.

As I opened the door of the phone booth, a black Ford LTD pulled into the convenience store. To my disbelief, the two guys I'd spied at the accident scene got out and went inside the store.

I reached in my car, grabbed the camera, hung it around my neck, and snapped a couple photos of their vehicle. Using my car as cover, I crouched down and got a clear picture of their rear bumper and license plate. About that time, the door swung open and out they walked.

I let my camera drop as I twisted toward my vehicle and pretended to check the air pressure of the tire. I sneaked a peek over my shoulder. The driver stood still, his eyes on me. Or maybe he was checking out my car. That happened a lot.

I rose as he took a step in my direction.

He pursed his lips. "Ooo-wee, is that a sixty-eight?"

Wishing I'd ditched the camera, I nodded. "Yes, sir, it is." He grinned and stepped closer, giving me a really good look at his face. Had he seen the car parked up there on the highway? A sensation like ants crawling up my spine sent a tremor through me.

"I've always wanted a Camaro. Looks like a custom paint job, too. What's she got under the hood?"

By this time, the passenger had trailed over. Willing myself to be calm, I forced a grin, popped the hood, and raised it. "Three-ninety-six."

The passenger, a shorter man with a rugged, dark complexion, leaned closer and ogled the engine. "I'll bet she purrs like a kitten."

There was an edge to his voice, a slight inflection. European, maybe? I rubbed the back of my neck and attempted a grin. "A bit more like a tiger."

The driver sucked air through his teeth. "Muscle car for sure. You're a lucky man. Must be a real pleasure to drive." He jerked his head toward their vehicle. "Speaking of which, we better hit the road, T."

T gave me a nod before turning away. "Thanks for the look-see, man."

I lowered the hood and pushed it closed. "No problem."

Back inside my car, I waited until they drove away before I pulled in a deep breath and blew it out. I was sure they were onto me. Good thing I'd taken off my press badge.

I decided to delay my other errand and head back to

the office. I wanted the prints developed asap.

Even if I didn't end up writing the story, I'd gathered some valuable info. I popped open the glove compartment and grabbed a licorice twist, my most recent substitution for a smoke.

As I drove and chewed, I wondered about the victims of that wreck. Who had they left behind? After checking in at work, I'd stop by the hospital. I knew a sweet little nurse who worked in the emergency room weeknights.

This time, I didn't have to force a grin.

CHAPTER THREE

Asheville, North Carolina
Lisa

I stared at the dark leaves of the nearby trees as Mr. Tobey spoke a few quiet words.

"I am the resurrection and the life. Whoever believes in me, though he die, yet shall he live, and everyone who lives and believes in me shall never die." His words echoed beneath the small, green tent, as though spoken into a deep canyon.

"Do you believe this?"

I wrenched my gaze away from the trees to look at him. Was he talking to me?

He closed the Bible and stepped forward, hand outstretched.

I allowed him to envelop my hand in his large, warm grip.

He didn't seem to expect an answer to his question. Good thing, because I had nothing. I wasn't sure whether I believed it or not. "Thank you, Mr. Tobey."

He responded with a smile and then bent his head to meet my gaze. "It's been our pleasure, Lisa. Mine and Thea's."

Thea slipped an arm around my waist and gave me a sideways hug.

Though I had only known them for three days, their genuine affection for me warmed my heart. I couldn't find the words to fully thank them for letting me stay with them, helping me through the funeral, holding my hand. For a few moments, the darkness receded.

Mr. Tobey straightened. "Is there anything else we can do for you?"

I forced myself to take a breath before shaking my head. "No, I don't think so." Then I lifted my gaze to his deep brown eyes. "I can't thank you enough."

"No need. We were happy to help." His lips formed a thin line as he nodded.

Thea pressed a gentle hand against my cheek. "If you ever need anything, you know where we are. You have our phone number. Don't hesitate to call."

I gave her my word. Emptiness filled my chest as they walked away. I hadn't realized how much I'd grown to appreciate them. I made a mental note to send them a thank-you card as soon as I arrived home.

I didn't notice Mr. Lewitt's approach until he appeared at my side. "We're ready to go, Miss Oliver, whenever you are."

After one last, long look at the dark metal caskets that held my parents, I turned and walked toward the black limousine that had brought me here.

The driver opened the door for me as Mr. Lewitt and I approached.

An overcast sky promised more rain in the forecast. I had no desire to drive home in the rain.

As my gaze lowered, my attention came to rest on a man, half-bent near a gravestone. It seemed almost as though he watched me.

The driver cleared his throat. I startled a bit, took my seat, and then nodded my thanks as he closed the door.

He and Mr. Lewitt carried on a quiet conversation in the front seat, giving me privacy to digest the morning's events. Mom and Dad would never have approved of a full-blown funeral with the twenty-four-hour wake and visitation followed by a formal service. But I could see now, all those things were more for the survivor than the deceased. Doing their service this way made more sense and saved money, but it left me empty, bereaved, and alone.

I recalled Mr. Tobey's quiet words, spoken over the caskets. *I am the resurrection and the life. Whoever believes . . . will live.*

Did I believe this?

A tear carved a slow path down my cheek. My parents had not been believers. They'd always encouraged me to find my own way in life.

"We've arrived, Miss Oliver."

With a start, I realized the car had stopped.

Mr. Lewitt opened my door, and I got out. He walked me to my car. "You'll be all right?"

I attempted a smile. "I'm used to flying solo, really."

He squared his shoulders and gave me one of those fatherly looks that made me feel like a five-year-old. "But not like this."

I suppose it was my solitariness that brought out the nurturing genes in many of those I met.

He opened my door. "Looks like rain's headed our way. I hope you're not planning to drive home today." He didn't need to tell me about the treacherous road.

I shook my head. "Only partway tonight." For the return trip, I intended to take the route Dad had driven, but in full daylight, lest I tempt fate. I preferred that no one knew about that, so I hadn't told the Tobeys, either.

It was curiosity and probably morose, but I needed to see the place where Dad drew his last breath.

Mr. Lewitt nodded. "God bless you, Miss Oliver."

Jake

My day hadn't gone as planned. After a short flirtation with Wendy, my favorite emergency nurse, I headed to the cemetery. She'd said there was going to be a private service at the grave site.

Now, I was really curious. Why hadn't they been shipped home? There wasn't even an obituary. Odd.

This wasn't the first time that I'd let my curiosity get the best of me. It would've been better if I'd never seen Lisa Oliver and never gotten a look at those big, sad eyes.

I would scarcely have called it a funeral, but I was able to watch them, while pretending to visit a headstone across the way. From my crouch, as I arranged some flowers in the vase there, I caught a glimpse of Lisa, the dead couple's daughter according to Wendy, as she climbed into the limo.

It was only a moment when our eyes met, but her gaze captured and held my attention. I couldn't seem to pull it away. It wasn't until the limo drove off that my mind cleared.

I had to learn more about Lisa Oliver and her family.

I waited outside the funeral home until Miss Oliver left in a little blue Volkswagen.

While waiting, I jotted down a quick description. "No more than twenty or twenty-one. Light brown hair, trim figure. Eyes—brown?" Not sure.

I pocketed the notepad and went inside.

I doubted whether I'd get any information out of the director, but it was worth a try. If nothing else, I'd gotten a last look at the lovely orphan, the make and model of her car, and her license plate number.

A pleasant middle-aged woman showed me to the funeral director's office. A nameplate on the man's desk identified him as S.J. Lewitt. I nodded a greeting as I entered.

"Mr. Lewitt, I'm Jake Bradley, a reporter with the Asheville Summary. I'm writing a follow-up story on the accident victims, kind of a human-interest piece."

He gave me a polite nod. "I'm sorry, young man. I can't give you any information, other than this." With one long finger, he slid a small brochure toward me.

I smiled and nodded as I picked up the order of service. "I understand. Thank you, sir."

I tucked the paper into my notepad and pocketed my pen.

Mr. Lewitt rose from his chair. "There was so little said about the accident in your paper, Mr. Bradley. I don't understand the need for a follow-up."

I shrugged, deciding for a change, to be honest. "I can't really explain it, sir. I just can't seem to let it go."

He tapped those long fingers against the desk as he gave me a knowing smile.

What? Did he think I was skirt-chasing? "The fact so little was said about it—it's kind of sad, don't you think? That young woman lost everything."

He nodded. "Perhaps where they're from, their local newspaper will publish a story." He offered his hand. "Nice to meet you, Mr. Bradley."

I shook his hand. "Thank you, sir. Have a nice day." My few minutes of research had yielded little information on the Olivers. They'd lived in Bybee, Kentucky for a short time, but that was the extent of it. More reason for me to dig deeper.

CHAPTER FOUR

Lisa

Rain fell overnight, leaving the pavement damp, but Dad's route was nearly deserted at that hour. It seemed most travelers chose the freeway, so I took my time. I had to admit. It was certainly a beautiful drive.

Except for the part about looking for the scene of a fatal accident that involved my parents.

As I drove, I fingered the rings on my necklace. The two narrow gold bands had been on my parents' fingers for almost twenty-five years. Mr. Lewitt had placed them in my palm before we left for the grave site. I'd promptly added them to the necklace Mom had given me, a gold locket containing hers and Dad's pictures.

Not much else remained of my parents' possessions.

The patrolman who'd first come upon the scene of the accident told Mr. Tobey the car had careened down an embankment and rolled into a rain-swollen stream. What little was left of what they'd packed in their classic Plymouth Satellite wagon fit in a single cardboard box, which Mr. Tobey had placed in the backseat of my car. The bag given to me at the hospital occupied the passenger's seat.

I could still see Mom's face reflecting her usual hopefulness over this move. They'd taken me out to my favorite restaurant for dinner. Afterward, we'd talked for over an hour, revisiting old memories, some funny, some poignant. We said goodbye outside my dorm.

In retrospect, Mom's hug seemed tighter, more deliberate than normal. Was that my imagination playing tricks?

Dad had been his typical jovial self. "See ya, kid. Take care of yourself, you hear? Don't let anyone take advantage of you." Then, he'd cupped the back of my head in his hand and pressed a kiss against my brow. Classic Dad.

Except for the depth of sorrow in his eyes.

I'd noticed it then but hadn't remarked on it. He never talked about himself and shied away from feelings.

Feelings weren't manly.

Another sharp curve gained my full attention. About halfway up a steep incline, damaged trees on the other side of the road caught my eye. A couple of cars following behind me made it impossible to stop or even slow down, so I kept going until I found a place to pull over. Once traffic cleared, I made a U-turn.

My heart thudded in my chest as I drove back down. I turned into a narrow road that could've been a driveway, about a hundred or so feet from the damaged trees. I pulled as far to one side as possible so someone could get by me if they needed to, parked, and got out. Other than the occasional passing car, it was eerily quiet, but that was probably just my impression.

I picked my way carefully through grass and mud to the site. Tire marks and deep trenches in the dirt proved that someone had indeed run off the road at this point. My pulse sped up when I took in the scene. Far below me, a thicket had been flattened all the way down to a rocky stream. This had to be the spot. If the hill had been less steep, I might have been tempted to climb down and take a look. I gripped a nearby tree trunk. Looking down made me dizzy.

A light crunch of gravel behind me sent shivers

shooting up my spine. When I turned, I saw a man in the uniform of a highway patrolman walking toward me. He looked the part, muscular and stern-faced.

"Is that your Volkswagen parked back there?"

I nodded. "Yes, sir."

"Are you having car trouble?"

"No, sir. I'm sorry, I just wanted to see where my father died." I swiped at an unexpected tear.

His expression softened. "They were your parents?"

I nodded.

"This is a dangerous stretch of road, ma'am. I'll walk you back to your car."

In other words, *Move along.* I was happy to comply.

He followed behind me. "I really am sorry, ma'am. I was the first officer on the scene."

I glanced over my shoulder. "So you're the one who talked to Mr. Tobey."

"Yes, ma'am. I intended to write you a letter. I spoke with your mother and stayed with her 'til the ambulance arrived. I hoped she'd make it. I was real sorry when I heard she'd passed."

Back at the car, I opened the door. "Thank you for telling me. I'm glad she had someone with her." My lips trembled as tears threatened again.

He removed his hat and held it in both hands. "She spoke of you. Said you're a student at Eastern Kentucky."

I couldn't help the smile. Mom had talked about me. "Yes."

"She said they left to protect you. Does that mean something to you?"

I crossed my arms over my chest to keep from shivering as ice water trickled through my veins. What had she meant by that? I shook my head. "I'm not sure."

"The last thing she said to me was, 'Keep her safe.'" He stood still a moment, watching me. "I suppose I could help you out a little. You shouldn't take this road. You'd be better off driving the interstate. We've had a lot of rain recently, and this old road is subject to rockslides."

I swallowed, then frowned, thinking about a change in my route. Would I have to go all the way back down?

He donned his hat. "If you have a map, I'll show you the closest on-ramp."

I reached inside my car and produced the map. He opened it and laid it on the hood, then pointed out an alternative route. "It's pretty easy to find. Once you get close, you'll see signs directing you." He stepped back while I gathered the map.

"Thank you, Officer." I slid into my seat and shut the

door.

He straightened his hat and started to walk away but doubled back. "It'll be easier if you just follow me to the turnoff. Once I turn, I'll pull over, but you can pass on by. After five miles or so, you'll see the interstate signs."

I followed along behind the officer's vehicle. He turned at a junction and pulled onto the side of the road. I passed by, raising my hand in farewell.

Was it a coincidence, meeting him at the scene of the accident, or all God's plan, as Mr. Tobey liked to say? I wasn't sure, but the patrolman's words chilled me to the bone.

She said they left to protect you.

Jake

If I had never seen Lisa Oliver's face, I possibly could have walked away from this and never looked back.

I ran my hands through my too-long hair and grimaced at the typewriter. Unfortunately, the very real pain reflected in her expression had lodged itself in my brain, and I couldn't seem to get past it.

Even a robbery at gunpoint couldn't hold my

attention. I'd only written four words of my latest assignment.

I leaned back in my chair and sighed. Good thing I loved a challenge. Otherwise, the lack of information about the ill-fated Olivers would make walking away a whole lot easier.

Those few facts I'd gleaned became beacons in the night, urging me on. My imagination kicked into high gear. A sense of urgency drove me.

A familiar voice brought me back to the present—my desk and the article I was supposed to have finished early this morning.

"Bradley. My office." Mr. Hamilton's growl was in rare form.

I blew out a sigh. *Great.* I didn't need more trouble. Would this be strike three?

Lucky chuckled and shook his head. "Nice knowing you, kid."

I scowled at him as I hurried to Hamilton's office.

He looked up as I entered. "Shut the door and sit down."

The last drop of hope flitted away as I closed the door. Steeling myself, I sat in the chair as if this was my office, and he was the one about to be sacked.

He wasn't impressed. "I haven't seen your assignment come across my desk."

"I'm nearly finished."

He huffed. "I just got off the phone with my friend, Sam. He said he talked to you yesterday. He seems to think you're working on a follow-up story about that couple killed last week on Route 25." He stopped talking and stared at me, waiting for my answer.

Sam had to be Mr. Lewitt. I hadn't spoken with anyone else except my nurse friend. And Wendy was no Sam.

I pressed my lips together and nodded. "I did say that, yes."

He sat back in his chair and crossed his arms over his chest. "Tell me what you know."

I removed my notepad and flipped it open. "Accident occurred just after two in the morning on Highway—"

Hamilton hit the desktop with his fist. "I know that part. Tell me what it is about this story that made you risk losing your job?"

I gulped in a breath. "When I scouted out the scene of the accident, two men showed up. At first, I thought they were detectives until I overheard their conversation. I think it's possible they were in some way involved—

maybe even responsible—for the fatality."

He sat forward. "You have their conversation in detail?"

"I do." I read through the transcript and then looked him in the eye. "They were searching for something in particular but didn't find it. One of them mentioned if they didn't make contact with their boss, he'd send the 'ankle-buster.' That led me to believe there's more to this story. Then, when I found out the couple left a daughter, now orphaned, I had to wonder if the girl might also be in danger."

Deep furrows etched Hamilton's brow. He eased back in his chair.

I kept my eyes on his face. Had I convinced him?

He turned toward the windows behind his desk. "Write up what you have. I'll take a look at it and let you know."

I took that as a dismissal and stood.

The squeal of his chair as he faced me again told me otherwise. "You know I don't like this sort of thing, Bradley. Bad etiquette. By rights, I should fire you and give this story to Tillman. But he didn't have the gumption to go after it."

My hand was on the doorknob when he stopped me

again.

"I think you're on to something, Bradley. And I think you're right, that girl's life could be in danger. You need to go to the police with this information. They need to know about those two guys." He tapped his desk. "But wait until after we get this in print."

CHAPTER FIVE

April 16, 1971
Eastern Kentucky University
Lisa

Little Blue and I made the return trip in record time. Little Blue was what Dad had dubbed my Volkswagen. He'd given me the car my senior year of high school. The memory sent a stab of pain to my heart.

What had happened to him? Why had Mom said they had to leave to protect me? Those questions and more had filled my thoughts all the way home.

I found my dorm room empty, which didn't surprise me since my roommate usually went home on weekends. I sat on my bed, gripping the plastic bag of personal effects. Mom's purse. Dad's billfold. Did they contain any clues?

Rather than igniting my curiosity, the question sickened my stomach. I wasn't ready to touch their belongings. I couldn't even look at them. My hands shook as I replaced the items and then stuffed the bag in the cardboard box rescued from the wrecked car. I hid the box in my closet to deal with later. Maybe after finals. Maybe when my heart hurt less, if such a time should come.

My footsteps echoed in the quiet hall as I walked to the pay phone. I needed to let the Tobeys know I'd made it home safely. Then I spent the rest of the weekend reading and studying to catch up on my work.

I dreaded my roommate's return. Since we lived in such close quarters, her questions couldn't be avoided. On top of that, she was a psyche major.

Shelby trounced in around six on Sunday evening. "I really don't get you." She plopped down crossed-legged on her bed, a book the size of Texas cradled on her lap. "You should take some time off. You need to process this."

I shook my head. "No way. I want to finish the year. I have to." Once finals were behind me, I could get away from here for a while.

"I'd be a basket case if my folks died. I can't even imagine it." Her eyes brimmed with unshed tears.

I turned away and stared out the window. "I am kind of numb. I guess that's my version of a basket case." I faced her again. "My parents raised me to be independent. Maybe they did too good a job."

She shook her head. "I've never known anyone quite like you, that's for sure."

I sat on my bed. "I do have one request. I hope you'll honor it. Please don't talk about it to anyone. I'd rather no one knew."

She shrugged. "Well, nobody's going to be thinking about anything other than passing finals, so I guess the timing is good." She rested her chin on her hands. "If you had more friends, it might be a problem."

I gave her a wry smile. It was true. I liked to think I kept my circles small. Intimate.

She opened her book and looked down at it, but I could tell she wasn't reading. She was still trying to analyze me.

"So, what will you say if anyone asks?"

I aimed my gaze at the wall. I was not a good liar. We both knew that. On that long drive between North Carolina and Eastern Kentucky, I'd come up with what I considered a really good line.

"If anyone asks, I can tell them my folks are all settled

in. Firmly planted in North Carolina soil."

She blinked.

I'd taken her by surprise.

Then she smacked me with a pillow. "Oh, my gosh, Lisa! You can't say that."

She was probably right. I shrugged. "Why not? It's true, sort of."

"You really are the strangest person I've ever met.

The darker the night, the brighter the stars, the deeper the grief, the closer is God.

Dostoyevsky's observation in *Crime and Punishment* haunted my nights. His words cut deeply, especially after that passage of Scripture Mr. Tobey had chosen for the burial service.

"Do you believe this?" His question had disturbed the dark waters of my soul that day. Did I believe in the existence of a higher power? A God who was close to those enduring grief?

Had my parents believed in something after all, or were their souls floating around in outer space? Dad told me aliens had seeded the earth. He'd always laughed afterward, so I'd never known whether he was joking or serious. Had he really believed that? Either way, I was sure Dad never planned on leaving so soon.

I couldn't sleep, so I studied.

Shelby eyed me as she dried her hair with a towel. "Oliver This isn't healthy. Maybe I can get you a session with my professor, or one of the counselors."

I shook my head. "I'm okay. Just working through some things." I couldn't tell her I was questioning the existence of God or that I was teetering toward a life of faith. She would do her best to talk me out of it.

She took a more humanistic approach to life. Not long after I'd met her, she'd declared, "There was never a magical creation, life evolved naturally, over time." Her ultra-pragmatic approach left no room for debate.

Though she dearly loved a good argument, I would not give her one. I was too tired.

Even so, I had no trouble focusing during my classes, and those extra study sessions sent my brain into overdrive.

Shelby worried that I would have a breakdown. "You'll probably crash as soon as you get through finals. I read that when people have something to keep them going, like an important job, or a child to raise, they often delay the grief process. But sometimes they end up burying their feelings . . ."

My attention left the building after that. I was still very much in the room and wishing to be anywhere else.

I lay down on my bed and faced the wall. Darkness descended over me. Shafts of gray light drew me forward until I stood beside a large body of dark green water, so still, it looked like a mirror. I admired the beauty until I noticed something floating on the surface. I waded out into the water, to get a closer look. An icy chill ran through me when I realized what it was. A body floated there with dead eyes staring at the sky, and mouth agape as though gasping for breath.

Terror sent a mad rush of adrenaline through me. My own heartbeat drowned out all other sounds. I tried to run, but only managed to stumble, and then fell into the water beside the body. Thrashing about, I struggled for control.

I woke when someone called my name.

Sitting upright in bed, I rubbed my face with my hands. Dim light filtered through the curtains at our window. I squinted at the clock. I'd managed to sleep until 5:10 a.m., but the dream had left me shaken.

No doubt, the suddenness of my parents' death had

brought the dream back to me. Was it possible my childhood nightmare had been a foreshadowing?

STILL WATER

CHAPTER SIX

Jake
Asheville, North Carolina

Sweat trickled down my back as I locked the door to
my third-floor apartment. I shifted my typewriter
case from beneath my left arm to my right hand and
dashed down the stairs. As usual, I was running late.

I had a meeting with my boss and then an interview
with a police detective. After those were out of the way, I
could hit the road.

Hamilton greeted me with his usual gruff bark, which
I ignored.

He'd been satisfied with my preliminary write-up of
the accident. I had to use a magnifying glass to find it in
Friday's edition, but it was a start. He'd approved a follow-

up story as well, though it meant I'd be out of the office for at least a month. Maybe that's why he'd approved it. He'd been trying to get rid of me for weeks. I quirked a smile at the thought as I took a seat in his office.

He slid a large, manila envelope across his desk. "I have your marching orders."

I picked it up and was about to open it when he stopped me with an uplifted hand.

"Not here. You need to get on the road. They're expecting you at ten. If you hurry, and don't run into any traffic jams, you may just make it."

I tucked the envelope under my arm and turned to go.

"Bradley?"

I looked over my shoulder.

He gave me a final nod. "Good luck to you."

"Thank you, sir."

"You better bring me a good story." He spun in his wooden seat back toward his phone.

"I hope to, sir." Not a good story, a great one. Why else would I feel so strongly about it? On my way out, I tried not to meet the gazes of any of my coworkers.

They all thought I'd been fired.

I reached the precinct office just before ten. Since it was Friday morning, I'd expected more activity at police headquarters, but only a few officers bent over their desks.

The officer on duty led me to a small, room furnished with a single, wooden table and three chairs. "Have a seat, Mr. Bradley. Someone will be right with you."

This was not at all what I'd expected. The place was funky in a bad way. A mixture of body odor and cigarette smoke assaulted my nostrils. And there was no telling what had caused that stain on the table.

Rather than taking a seat, I paced and tried not to look at myself in the mirrored, one-way window. After what seemed hours, I heard footsteps approaching.

The door opened, but it was not the man I was supposed to meet. Instead of Detective Scott, a man in a gray suit entered, closing the door behind him. He may have been the most ordinary man I'd ever met, but his eyes showed intelligence. He held a black folder in one hand and a recorder in the other. After placing both articles on the table, he faced me, his hand outstretched.

"Mr. Bradley? I'm Agent Zach Farrow, FBI."

I'd already figured that one out. His closely cropped hair screamed military, but the nondescript gray suit, white shirt and striped tie reminded me of Special Agent Tom Colby from that *FBI* television show. Mom never missed that show.

He opened the folder and removed what looked like a form. Then he leveled his gaze at me. "I hope you don't mind if I record our conversation?"

That was usually my line. "No, sir."

A shadow passed over his expression. Did he think I was being flippant?

He switched on the recorder and for a few seconds, the only sound was the swish of the tape in the reels.

"Please state your name for the record."

And so it began. After giving my name, I began answering his questions.

"What is your occupation?"

"Crime reporter for the *Asheville Summary*, first year on the job."

"And why was a crime reporter at the scene of a car accident?"

I shrugged. "A hunch. Thought it might be a good human-interest piece."

He eyed me.

I resisted the impulse to squirm in my seat.

"All right then, tell me exactly what you observed at the scene."

Just the facts, Jake. No conjectures.

His gaze never left my face as I told him what I had witnessed at the scene and heard from the two men who had arrived while I was there. Using my notepad, I checked to make sure I had not forgotten a single detail. If a young woman's life was at stake, I meant to do whatever I could to help.

Agent Farrow wrote notes on the paper in front of him.

I glanced at my watch. We'd been at it for two hours.

He looked at me. "So, you got a good look at those two? Would you recognize them if you saw them again?"

I nodded. "I believe so, yes."

"Can you describe them to a sketch artist if necessary?"

"Yes." Agent Farrow shut off the recorder and gathered the papers that had become scattered on the table. "I appreciate your thoroughness, Mr. Bradley."

I tried to appear nonchalant. "I hope it helps." Since I had been so cooperative, would he return the favor? "I know you probably can't talk about the case."

He glanced up at me. "You'll do well to abandon any interest you have in this case, Mr. Bradley. There's no story here. Nothing of any literary value, whatsoever."

He may as well have issued a challenge. I nodded.

"Am I free to go?"

After a short staring contest, he held out his card. "If you should come across information pertinent to this case, give me a call."

I accepted the card. "I'll do that." I didn't move until he did. Being closer to the door, I opened it and stepped aside for him to pass through.

He walked out but waited for me to catch up. "I know you're after a story, but believe me, there's nothing to this. Just two bullies who forced an innocent couple off the road on a rain-soaked highway."

I nodded. "You're probably right." *Yeah, that's why the cops called in the Feds.*

I left the office more determined than ever to snoop out the facts surrounding this case. That was no random act of violence by two bullies, it was a deliberate chase with an unexpected ending.

CHAPTER SEVEN

Jake
On the Road

My interview with Agent Farrow had spurred a memory. During my two-year stint in the Navy, I'd served as an office assistant to a judicial advocate. I'd made some good friends in that office. Among them was Crandall "Cran" Roberts, who'd recently passed the Virginia bar. I decided this was a good time for me to pay a visit to my old buddy.

He'd been one of the best researchers in the JAG office. He'd taught me a thing or two, as well, and I'd helped him out on occasion.

After a quick stop to top off my gas tank, I headed out but took a roundabout route. An odd feeling, similar to a cold hand clenching the back of my neck, kept me casting glances in the rear-view mirror. I wasn't sure whether I expected to see that black LTD, or the Feds, but I had no doubt I could out drive either. Even though I preferred not to.

Once I hit the open road, I rolled down the window and settled back. A side-trip to Virginia would at least throw the Feds off my trail, if they even cared what I was up to.

I spent the night in a motor inn outside Greensboro, North Carolina, where I mapped out the rest of my trip. I scheduled in a couple of days in Richmond, depending on what Cran had going on.

I opened the manila envelope and removed the file Hamilton had placed inside. Copies of the original accident report, preliminary report from the county medical examiner, and a handwritten note from Hamilton.

"Marching orders," he'd called them.

The note was short and sweet. *A weekly "Jake On the Road" column for the Sunday magazine, along with progress updates on the Oliver case. Give me a reason to keep you.*

I lay down on the bed and sighed. "Lord, is it always going to be this hard?"

Lisa's face came to mind with those sad eyes that pierced my soul. "Lord, help me find a way to protect her."

Was that really what I wanted, to help Lisa Oliver, or was it some sort of egotistical hero complex?

Seeking recognition, a catch-22 for journalists. I grimaced into the darkness before finishing my prayer. "If it's Your will, Father, help me help her."

Before dawn, I was back on the road. Maybe it was my military training that kept me on high alert. I couldn't seem to shake the feeling I was being tailed. Leaving before light was out of character for me, though, and might give me an edge.

Rain pelting me in sheets wasn't on my agenda, but it could also help. I exited the interstate and crossed the state line via a country road that rivaled the scene of the accident outside Asheville.

Near the Richmond city limits, I located a mom-and-pop grocery and pulled off the road. I used the pay phone to call information for Cran's number. The operator connected the call for me.

My old friend's secretary answered after one ring with a formal, "Office of Crandall Roberts. May I help you?"

"Hello, this is Jake Bradley. I'm an old friend of Mr.

Roberts's. Is he available?"

"Mr. Roberts has a busy schedule today, Mr. Bradley. Can I tell him you called?"

"I'm on long distance. Would it be possible for me to speak to him for just a moment? I served with him in the Navy. We worked together in a JAG office."

"Hold one moment, sir."

"Jake?" Cran's jovial voice bled through the line. "You in town?"

"Almost. I was hoping to steal a couple of hours from you if you have the chance."

He laughed. "I just happened to have time available to meet later this afternoon. You're not in any trouble, are you? Not been stalking any new chicks?"

I laughed. "No trouble." Not yet anyway. "Nothing like that."

I made a note of the address and hung up.

A few hours later, I spotted my friend standing just inside the restaurant he'd chosen. Cran hadn't changed much. He still wore his hair trimmed short and he'd stayed in shape.

His grip was strong as we shook hands. "Hey, old man, how are you?" He nodded to the restaurant's hostess, a slim, middle-aged woman in a black dress. She led us to a booth near the back of the room, dropped a couple menus in front of us and retreated.

From my side of the booth, I smiled at Cran. "Who are you calling old?" I opened the menu. "What's good here?"

"You have to try their ribeye. It's amazing."

After placing our orders, I got down to business. Leaving out the fact that I hadn't been assigned the story in the beginning, I related the facts surrounding the accident.

He stirred more sugar into his iced tea than I'd expect to find in a birthday cake, and then he took a sip as I finished my dump of information. "Sounds like a challenge. I'm sure you're up for it, but I have to wonder, is she pretty?"

I frowned into his astute gaze. "Is who pretty?"

He leaned forward. "Come on, Jake, I know you."

I sat back. "Like I said, the couple had a daughter, who is now an orphan. I've never met her."

He persisted. "But you've seen her."

I nodded. "Yes, I've seen her. From a distance, but I don't know her. She's a student at Eastern Kentucky. She went back home right away."

He cracked a wry smile. Did he believe me? I wasn't sure. He knew me, all right.

"So, what are you expecting of me? How can I help you?"

Down to business. Very Cran of him. "I'm coming up empty on my background checks. You're the king of research. I hope you have some ideas."

Our conversation paused when the waitress returned with our meals. The delicious aroma of the seared meat left me salivating like a mastiff. I was hungry, and my first bite was sheer delight. Cran was right about that steak, it was worthy.

Cran cut a bite of meat and dipped it in mushroom gravy. "Do you have a room for the night?"

I nodded. "Not far from here. I figured I'd need a couple of days."

He shrugged. "At least. We'll see what happens. You come to my office tomorrow morning. We can at least start on it before you have to take off." He bit back a grin. "Are you headed to Kentucky next?"

"Just so happens, that's my next stop."

By the end of our first session, we had three years' worth of addresses for the Olivers, and ownership info on the black LTD, Niko Petrov. I was in no hurry to follow up on that.

I examined the DMV form Cran had given me. "Think I'll leave that one to the Feds."

Cran stood looking out of his office windows, hands stuffed in his pockets. "With a name like Petrov, I tend to agree. They could be Bulgarian mafia. Or tied to the Soviets somehow. Keep a safe distance, buddy." He turned to face me. "All these moves worry me. We haven't found military records that match, or personal history. They never stayed anywhere longer than a few months. Was this couple on the run?"

"That's how it looks, but it could be perfectly innocent. He could've been out of work, looking for a change from driving or just looking for a change period. Their daughter was off at college, so maybe they were taking the opportunity to find a more permanent situation."

Cran nodded. "Maybe that's all it is. If you can locate the daughter and talk to her, you may find out." He sat in his chair, leaned back, and stared at the ceiling. "I'm wondering what your story will be about. What's your angle? Why are you so interested in this one?"

I leaned forward, my elbows on my knees. I'd had the

same questions circling for days. "I can't really tell you, right now, because honestly, I don't know. I feel a little bit like a dog chasing its tail. What in the world will I do with it when I catch it?"

I grinned and then touched my forehead. "It's something in here." Then I laid my hand flat over my heart. "And in here. This is something I have to pursue. I just know."

CHAPTER EIGHT

Jake

Cran's question cycled through my mind for hours as I drove along the dusty backroads of rural Virginia. It had been two weeks since the accident. My research had yielded no answers. I could not explain this obsession with the Olivers.

The first night on the road, I set up my tent in a small campground in the Blue Ridge Mountain region. Raindrops pattered against the canvas overnight. By morning, the sky had cleared, revealing the natural beauty of my surroundings. I grabbed my fishing pole and tackle box.

Looking all touristy with a camera slung around my neck, I made my way to a wide spot along a mountain stream and cast a line in. I anchored the rod between a couple of rocks and snapped some photos.

Upriver, a fisherman stood waist-deep, sending out expert casts and soon caught a good-sized trout. I focused a closeup on his catch.

Noticing me, he held the fish high for another shot.

I picked my way along the shoreline as he bent to stow his catch in a bucket of water. Securing the lens cap in place, I greeted him. "Hope you don't mind me snapping photos."

"Not at all. Nice camera you have there. You a photographer by trade?"

"No, I have a travel column in the *Asheville Summary*. I use the photos to help me write my articles. Helps to jog my memory, you know."

He nodded. "Makes sense."

I pointed to his rod and reel. "You're good at that."

"Should be. I'm a professional. Make the rounds of local, and not-so-local sport fishing competitions."

Professional. The word struck a chord in my memory. I set it aside for a moment. "A sport fisherman? Interesting. So, this is practice?"

"Might say that. Or you might call it breakfast." He grinned.

I stepped away. "Well, I'll leave you to it. I just wanted to make sure you were okay with being photographed."

He paused. "Would you be able to send me a copy of the photos?"

"Sure, I can do that." I tugged at my ever-present pad and pen.

He tucked the rod under one arm, stuck two fingers in the breast pocket of his fishing vest, and pulled out a small, white card. "You can mail them to this address."

I barely suppressed a whistle as I read, *Major General Elton Q. Lewis.* I was in the presence of greatness. "Major General, pleased to meet you, sir. I'm Jake Bradley."

He gripped my outstretched hand. "The pleasure's mine, young man. I'm retired and enjoying every minute of it. Be sure to include a bill for printing and mailing the photos."

I had no intention of charging a retired Major General for a couple of pieces of paper. I nodded and took my leave.

Back downstream, I picked up my fishing pole and tackle, and trudged back to my campsite. I wouldn't be enjoying a fresh trout for breakfast but had a good start on my next column. After jotting down a few notes, I packed my gear and headed out.

Miles of dusty roads had rendered the color of my car unrecognizable, so I relaxed a bit and used the time to chew on the memories sparked by something the Major General said. *Professional.* One of those two men at the crash site had used that word to describe William Oliver.

He was a professional what—driver? A truck driver, yes, but a professional truck driver still may not be able to maneuver a station wagon over rain-slick roads in the midst of a downpour. I had a feeling that guy meant something different by his use of that word.

What if Oliver was a professional driver of another sort? What if he raced cars, or—another memory tugged at my thoughts—a story a while back about a guy arrested for drug running. *Thunder Road* was not just a fictional tale, and it wasn't only historical, according to the article I'd read. And then, Cran had warned, that Petrov guy could be connected to the mafia.

Outside a small café, I called Cran's office and left a message. "Look for a story about a drug runner arrested in North Carolina last year. I'm on the road but will check back in a couple of days."

Cran's secretary probably thought I was a nutcase.

I drove for two more days, tent-camped in the mountains overnight. On the third day, I had a run-in with a black bear. He was only interested in the bologna sandwich I'd made for lunch. He was welcome to it. I jumped into the car and hit the road again.

In dire need of a shower and a good night's sleep, I stopped at a small motor inn outside Pikeville, Kentucky. Early the next morning, I took a walk through the scenic town which rested in a valley surrounded by the Appalachian Mountains.

I enjoyed a true country breakfast and talked with a direct descendant of one of the original McCoys, known for their infamous feud with neighboring Hatfields. Before leaving town, I roughed out two more columns to finalize when I had the opportunity.

I was in coalmine country. Area homes bespoke poverty though the actual history of the place was a bit more colorful. Paintsville, Kentucky had gotten its name from native-American art painted on debarked trees, according to the mayor. He seemed eager for me to write one of my travel posts about the town.

"The first recorded name was Paint Lick Station," he said. "It was a trading post."

I wrote down the information. "I imagine hunting was

good in those days, with a salt lick nearby."

"Yes, sir, and it still is when a man has the time to hunt."

Looking around the area later, I figured hunting was a great way to supplement slim wallets. The Appalachian region boasted much natural beauty, but poverty abounded.

After Paintsville, the mountains rolled out into foothills. The valleys widened into fertile pastureland, dotted with cattle, sheep, and horses. And my time on the road was coming to an end.

I had three rural addresses to check, searching for information on the Olivers. Then I'd head to Richmond and Eastern Kentucky University in time for classes to end.

CHAPTER NINE

Lisa

I'd heard mourning manifested itself in different ways.

Rather than depression or deep sadness, I seemed to be on an emotional high. My energy levels soared. But when the last class ended, all my gumption left. I wanted to find a dark corner, park there, and allow myself to grieve.

I picked up my mail on the way back to my room. A package had arrived for me. It was the size of a shoe box and wrapped in brown paper. The return address was a familiar one. I carried it back to my dorm room and set it on the bed.

The last place Mom and Dad had lived was a tiny cottage in nearby Bybee, Kentucky. The cottage had at one time been a gatekeeper's residence for a large estate. The present owner was an ancient little woman who had always wandered down to the cottage when I visited.

Even before I unwrapped it, I knew what it contained. Mom always left something behind. She'd gotten the idea from a book she'd read. Mom loved to read.

"We must always leave something behind, sweetie," she'd say. "Something of ourselves. Something we've touched."

I hadn't understood at the time, but she'd been quoting Ray Bradbury in *Fahrenheit 451*. Funny how the thing we left behind usually belonged to me.

I swiped at tears as I tore away the brown wrapping paper to reveal the familiar pink and white shoe box. When I removed the lid, my heart broke and so did the dam I'd built to harness my emotions.

That little box held my entire life. Photographs from my childhood, school pictures, and class photos.

I paused to blow my nose. Why on earth would Mom have left those behind?

Though it was late in the day, I packed my belongings. Shelby would party all night, so now was a good time for me to split.

Over the years, I had become an expert car-packer.

Car-stuffer may have been a better term. Once every square-inch of the interior was filled, including the luggage area beneath the rear window and the trunk space under the hood, I lifted my suitcases onto the luggage rack. At this point, a couple guys I knew from class stopped to assist me.

"Sneaking off without saying goodbye, Oliver?"

I shook my head at the sound of Shelby's voice. "I left you a note."

She stepped closer as the guys tied the ropes to secure my belongings on top of the car. "Just tell me you're not running away."

I thanked the guys before turning to face my roommate. "I'm not running away. I have to find somewhere to live, and I'll need a job to support myself. Lexington's my best chance of that. The sooner I get started, the better."

"You could come home with me. My parents spend most of the summer somewhere else anyway."

I needed a break from everyone, especially Shelby. I shook my head. "I appreciate the offer, but ..."

She tilted her head back, a habit of hers that always preceded the pronouncement of a diagnosis. "You need to talk to someone, Lisa."

"This is my way of handling it, Shelby. Trust me."

"Well, you have my home number. Call me if you need to talk."

I nodded. "I will. Lexington's not far. Maybe you can visit."

She smiled. "Maybe so. See you in the fall?"

I nodded. "See you in the fall." I hoped, with all my heart.

After a quick walk-through back in our dorm room, I made the final trek to the car. I drank in the sights and sounds of our campus, dressed in spring green and dotted with splashes of colorful blooms. This was the third year I'd made this journey, but somehow, this time felt different. More final.

Heavy-hearted, I pulled out of my parking spot. I hadn't succeeded at a stealthy retreat, but at least Shelby hadn't tried to delay my departure.

Maybe I was more like Dad than I liked to admit, always on the run. I sat at the last stop light in town and wondered which way to turn. I'd told Shelby that I was going to Lexington. I put on my blinker and turned in that direction.

A little while later, I arrived at the outskirts of Lexington, where the neon lights of a small motor inn beckoned. Sleep would help. Well-rested, I could come up with a plan.

The tiny room in the motor inn held little appeal except for the bed.

I woke several hours later to the sound of slamming doors and loud voices. After a quick trip to the bathroom, I switched on the television, turned the volume down, and went back to bed, hoping for another hour or so of sleep.

The next wake-up call was a wailing siren. *City life.*

When I sat up on the side of the bed, the dark cloud descended again. I wanted to curl up in a fetal position and stay there. I took in the room.

"This is not the kind of place you want to linger." I pushed my fingers through my hair. "A few hours into my solitary venture and I'm already talking to myself." I got up and headed to the bathroom.

A shower helped. Clean and dressed, I checked out of the motel. Just down the street, I found a café open for breakfast. The coffee was on the strong side, but it was hot and plentiful. While I waited for my food, I examined my checkbook. Good thing I'd worked a part-time job last semester. I'd managed to save a little money. With that and what was left from the last check Mom and Dad had deposited in my account, I would be all right for a while. A short while.

And I was on my own. Just like my parents before me, I was an orphan. Only thing was, they'd had each other. I had no one.

The waitress returned with a fragrant plate of food and set it in front of me. "Here you go, darlin'. Looks like you could use a good, warm meal. I'll be right back to freshen up your coffee."

After filling my cup, she gave her attention to the other patrons. I allowed my thoughts to wander, but my mind kept circling back to the fact that my folks had left me nothing, other than those few personal effects and the box of my childhood. And then there were the contents of that box from their vehicle. I'd given the items a cursory inspection, but they'd left no clue where to find whatever money Mom and Dad might have left behind.

The certified check Mom sent every quarter since I started college nearly three years ago paid tuition, lodging, and books. According to admissions, she had already paid for the semester next fall. Had that been the end of it? What would I do after that?

My folks hadn't trusted banks. When I was little, Mom

had stuffed change into a coffee can in the back of the fridge. That stash had provided for my needs and also a few non-necessities, like a bicycle and a pair of roller skates. Dad never knew about it because she always made the purchases while he was away.

Maybe, I needed an attorney. One I could trust. At least that had been Mr. Lewitt's advice. He seemed to think I was a little lamb in a field of wolves. I knew what he meant. On my own, I'd be fair bait for predators. Panic fluttered in my chest. I had no friends to speak of. No family.

My introverted parents hadn't made life easy for me.

STILL WATER

CHAPTER TEN

Jake

I crawled out of the one-man tent I'd erected the night before. The small fishing campground didn't have many other campers this time of year. The weather was too unpredictable so early in May. I stretched and yawned. It wasn't the best accommodation, but it was cheap. Until I could manage to send in a few more travel posts, I was definitely on a budget.

I stowed the tent and sleeping bag, and then drove to a nearby service station where I could shave and freshen up. The attendant pointed me in the direction of a small café. While I chowed down on a big country breakfast, I took out my map and planned the next couple of days.

So far, I'd checked out two of the Olivers' former

residences, finding similar stories at both. I couldn't really call it a pattern yet. The owners of both locations reported that the couple left without notice in the middle of the night. One owner said they seemed a little odd.

I had no trouble finding Bybee, Kentucky, since it was only about eight miles from Richmond, home of Eastern Kentucky University. Bybee was nestled in a region known as the knobs in Madison County. Every state I'd recently visited had a Madison County. Most also had knobs. I assumed it was an Appalachian thing to call them knobs and ridges instead of just hills.

When I noticed Drowning Creek Road on the map, I ran my finger along it, looking for Drowning Creek. Intriguing name. I followed it to the point where it emptied into the Kentucky River. Would I have time to make the physical drive? I had two good reasons for doing so. I was curious to see the region, and it might make a good subject for one of my weekly articles. Also, I had it on good authority that the small house the Olivers had rented was located on that road. Their legal address had been a P.O. Box, so it had taken some extra work to track down the physical address.

My curiosity won. After leaving the café, I found Drowning Creek Road and followed it to the end, which was literally the Kentucky River, then turned around. I had to admit, this was some beautiful country. It was like driving through a park.

Headed back toward Bybee, I found the cottage with a For Sale sign in the yard. A gravel lane beside the cottage wound up a small knob to a larger house. White fences bordered the lane and outlined several acres of wide green space where horses grazed. I parked in the adjacent driveway and got out, intending to look around. The red brick house seemed sturdy, though it was at least a half century old. It boasted a wide front porch and a screened-in back porch that overlooked the pasture. It was a bit too close to the road for my taste, but there didn't seem to be much traffic.

I hadn't been there long when I noticed a golf cart headed down from the big house on the knob. I held my ground as it approached. A petite woman, I'd guess to be in her seventies, sat behind the wheel. She was dressed for a garden party, but her white hair seemed a bit unkempt.

Gravel flew when she hit the brake. Her hands gripping the wheel, she leaned forward. "Are you here about the house?"

Mama had taught me not to lie, but I'd chosen a

profession that encouraged me to push the limits to get a story. I nodded. "Thought I'd take a look at it before calling the Realtor. It seems small."

She nodded. "It is small but efficient. It's been a rental for years. My son finally convinced me to sell it. He thinks I can't take care of it anymore." Still seated in the cart, she offered her hand. "Nelda Reardon."

I shook her hand. "Jake Bradley." Nodding toward the house, I asked, "Are there problems, then?"

She slid off the seat and stood. The afternoon sun at her back lit her white hair, giving it an angelic glow. She pointed at the roof. "Not anymore. You'll notice it has a new roof. And the pipes were updated, just last year." She waved me forward. "Come on in. I think you'll be pleasantly surprised."

I stuck my hands in my pockets and trailed behind her. "Was it difficult to keep it rented?"

She crinkled her nose. "Not until recently. These days, it seems folks prefer to buy a trailer and set it where they like. Have their own place, rather than rent." She swung the door open and stepped inside.

The wood floors had been polished to a high sheen. The place smelled a bit musty, but that was probably due to age and being closed up. I looked around the small front room. A red brick hearth held a potbellied stove, which was probably the only heat.

"There are two bedrooms," she said. "And a lovely view from all the windows."

I strode into the small kitchen and tried to imagine Lisa here, enjoying a meal with her parents. Had she visited often? I opened a couple of the drawers and found them clean, but empty. Same with the cabinets. For good measure, I checked below the sink. Good idea to check out the plumbing if one was interested in a property.

I turned back to the owner. "It seems to be well cared for."

"Yes, it was. The last renters didn't stay long, only a few months, but they took good care of it. The fellow was right handy. He's the one who hung the swing on the front porch. I sure hated to lose them." Her eyes took on a faraway look. "They were a bit odd. They didn't talk much. Then they up and left. Didn't give a notice. Here one day, gone the next. Left a note on the door that I was to keep the deposit, they didn't need it." She glanced up at me. "Here I am chattering away, taking up your valuable time."

I did my best to reassure her. "Oh, I'm not in a rush."

She turned and walked back into the front room. With any luck, she'd tell me more about the former tenants.

Instead, she led me through the two small bedrooms. "I know it's not much of a house but it's a fine size for a single man, or maybe a couple with no children." She aimed a pointed look at me.

After peeking into a small closet, I gazed out the window, killing time. I figured she was trying to ascertain my marital status. "I'm definitely single but I'm really not looking for myself. A friend of mine is hoping to find a place in the country." This was not a lie. I did have a friend like that.

A slight frown troubled her brow. "I see. There's only a quarter of an acre that goes with the house. Do you think maybe it's too small?" She walked out onto the porch.

"Probably. He needs room for friends and family to visit."

After locking the door, she laid a blue-veined hand on the back of the swing. "That former tenant of mine, she liked to sit out here of a morning. It is a pleasant spot with a fine view of the hills." Her eyes took on a faraway look again. "I do love it here."

"It's a pretty place." I nodded toward the pasture. "Those are some fine horses."

She looked up at me and smiled. "They're my tenants, too. Their owners pay me well for their care, so I do my best to keep them happy. Well, sir, I hope you don't mind, but I need to get back up the hill." She stuck out her hand. "It's been a pleasure, Mr. Bradley."

As the little woman drove the cart toward home, I jotted down a couple of things she had said that interested me. She'd called her former tenants odd. They'd kept to themselves, and then left without notice. It fit. She must have been talking about the Olivers.

STILL WATER

CHAPTER ELEVEN

Jake

I rolled into Richmond, Kentucky just after noon. With Cran's help, I had managed to obtain Lisa Oliver's address, so I headed straight there. The campus was a busy place with droves of students packing up to go home. Lucky them.

I'd already cruised through, looking for the blue beetle. No luck, so I found a parking spot and pulled into it. With all the activity, I went unnoticed as I entered the building and strolled down the corridor.

I found the room and knocked on the door. The girl who opened it was definitely not Lisa. The petite blond was cute in a mousey kind of way. She had that gypsy style of hairdo all the girls liked these days. Gold, wire-rimmed glasses sat on the bridge of her nose, a little past the comfort zone, in my opinion.

She pushed the glasses into place and met my gaze. "Who are you?"

"Jake Bradley. I'm looking for Lisa Oliver."

She shook her head. "You're too late. She left yesterday."

"Yesterday?"

A smile lit her eyes. "She didn't waste any time."

"Did she say where she was going?"

"If she did, I wouldn't tell you, Jake Bradley. I've never heard her mention you."

"I'm a friend of a friend."

"Well, she didn't say, exactly."

I gave her a slow nod as I constructed my next sentence. I wasn't sure how much this girl knew. I relaxed my stance. If this was Lisa's roommate, she could be a good source of info.

"We, uh, my friend hasn't heard from her, you know, since her folks died. She's on her own, so we wanted to make sure she has somewhere to go, among friends who care about her."

She lowered her eyes and shrugged. "I tried that, too. Even offered to bring her home with me. She refused.

Typical Lisa. She told me she was headed to Lexington, where she could find a better summer job." She lifted her head. "Well, Jake Bradley, I don't want to be rude, but I have to finish packing."

I hesitated, weighing my words carefully. "It probably wouldn't do any good to ask you to call me if you hear from her, would it?"

She looked me up and down, gave a cute little laugh, and shook her head. "It would not, friend of a friend."

"I thought not. Well, it was nice meeting you, uh—?"

She shook her head and smiled. "Lisa's roommate."

"Right. Nice meeting you, Lisa's roommate."

I headed out of the building. I could've turned on the charm and won her over. But that could backfire. My gut told me it wouldn't work on this one, anyway. She was a little too quick with the snappy answers.

Lisa

A quick drive around Lexington landed me in front of an older, white house with an "Apartment for Rent" sign out front. I knocked on the door.

The owner was a short, stout middle-aged man

named Ray. "Just put that sign out today. Rent's reasonable. We get a lot of students here, which is why it's empty." A silver tabby followed along behind him as he led the way up an outside staircase. He brushed the cat aside and opened the door. "That's Jax. She's a pest, but she won't bother anything."

I stepped inside. Empty was right. It was unfurnished, except for a stove and a fridge.

"It's an efficiency, all one room." He stayed on the landing, allowing me to look around.

I liked the number of windows that provided natural light and afforded a view of the quiet, tree-lined neighborhood. The linoleum tiled floor had been recently waxed and the rest of the room looked and smelled clean. I crossed to the small bathroom and switched on the light. Satisfied, I turned it off again and joined Ray on the landing. "Do you require a deposit?"

"Rent's seventy-five dollars a month. I usually ask for a month's rent in advance, so that would be a hundred and fifty." His brow furrowed as though he expected me to balk at the price.

"Can I pay a hundred now, and the rest in a couple of weeks?" If I could find a decent job, the rent was certainly doable. I didn't mind the lack of furniture.

He nodded. "A hundred's fine. When will you move in?"

"Now if that's all right. I just moved out of my dorm at EKU."

"Got a job yet?"

"I'll have one soon."

He nodded again before heading down the stairs. "That's the spirit. Well, let me know if you need any help."

Though I had so few things, moving in required an infinite number of trips up those stairs. Afterward, I headed to find a nearby grocery store. I found a *Fred's* where I could purchase a few household necessities like pans. I looked at dishes and flatware, but that could wait. Paper plates and plastic utensils would get me through.

One of the many things Dad had taught me was how to survive on very little. And never go anywhere without a sleeping bag. *You just never knew when you were going to need one.*

First thing Monday morning, I found my way back to the Bluebird Café for a much-needed cup of coffee. On the way in, I bought a newspaper, intending to begin my job search.

The same waitress smiled at me from across the room. "I'll be right with you, darlin'. Would you like coffee?"

"Yes, please."

She brought a cup and a pot of coffee, set the cup in front of me and filled it. "You take cream, right?"

When I nodded, she set a small pitcher of cream on the table.

"I'm Trudy. What can I get you today?"

"I'll have the two-egg plate. Eggs over easy."

"No meat?"

"No, thank you."

"All right, it'll be right up."

I turned to the want ads and skimmed the columns for something interesting, but my heart wasn't really in it. A sip of coffee calmed my nerves. When I set it down, I stared into the cup. The thought of being on my own, completely alone, sent a wave of panic over me. I forced a deep breath and slowly blew it out before taking another sip.

Trudy brisked by, serving her other patrons.

I watched her, hoping to refocus my thoughts long enough to stop the panic. There were narrow blue stripes in the fabric of her uniform I hadn't noticed before. I'd assumed it was white. The blue of her apron matched the stripe. Her smile greeted another customer who looked like a farmer, dressed in overalls.

A crash of pottery brought my attention to a busboy clearing a table near the window.

Trudy stopped back by to freshen my coffee. She glanced at the paper on the table. "Looking for a job, huh? What can you do?"

My English major probably wouldn't garner me a great position, so I chose not to mention it. "I've minored in business at EKU. I'd like to find an office job." I was thinking the pay would be better than waiting tables.

When she returned with my eggs and toast, she sat in the chair across from me, took out her pad, and scribbled on it. "My brother, Marty, works at an engineering firm. He told me they're hiring office help for the summer. Maybe they'd have something you could do. And it's not far." She tore off the slip of paper and pushed it toward me. "You got a place to live?"

I nodded. "Over off Clay's Mill."

She stood, lifted the steaming coffee pot, and refilled my cup. "Good deal. I wish you the best."

I still perused the want ads, circling several that

looked promising. I needed a job right away if I was going to survive on my own. It wasn't just the rent, I'd have to eat, too. And there would be other expenses, like gas in my car so I could drive around looking for work.

I ate slowly, in no hurry to leave the company of others, which was odd for me. I was usually content to be on my own but that was when I had a choice. My empty apartment held no appeal.

I folded the newspaper, grabbed my purse, and headed to the cash register where a young woman rang me up. I counted my change then returned to the table and left a quarter and a nickel for Trudy.

As I was leaving, she called out, "Let me know if you get that job."

On a hunch, I stopped at a nearby phone booth and called the number on Trudy's note.

CHAPTER TWELVE

Jake

*O*n the night of April 12th, William Oliver and his wife, *Roberta, perished when their vehicle left the road on Highway 25. There was no write up in the paper other than an incident report. There was not even an obituary written for the couple.*

My opening article had ended with a question and a promise.

Who were they? That's what I hope to find out.

William, *Bill* Oliver. Roberta, *Bobbi* Oliver. Where were they from? Who killed them, and why?

I lifted my fingers from the typewriter keys and ran them through my hair. I had pages of notes. The words should come easily but they did not.

I got up and strode to the window, a trip I'd made several times already. There was nothing to look at, nothing to take my mind off my present situation. Stuck.

Lisa Renee Oliver.

Her face haunted my dreams, yet I'd never even spoken to her. I needed to remedy that. Until I could talk to her, I had no story.

I hadn't counted on the girl already having moved out of her dorm. She'd left on Friday, right after her last finals. Who does that?

I had already sent two more articles via *Western Union*, so there was no rush to get back out on the road.

On a whim, I picked up the telephone book and flipped to the yellow pages. I found *The Guardian* and my friend, Albert Russell. I dialed his number.

"The Guardian. How may I help you?"

I chuckled. "Hey, Russell, it's Jake Bradley. You answer your own phone, huh?"

"Far out. Bradley, how have you been, man?"

"I'm actually in Lexington for a while. I write a travel column for the *Asheville Summary*, so I'm checking out the local scenery."

"Groovy, man. Why don't you swing by sometime? I'm on my way out right now, but I'm here most days. How about breakfast in the morning? I have a fave spot across the street from my office."

"Sounds good. I found you in the directory, so I have the address. What time?"

"Eight o'clock all right with you?"

"You got it, man." How easily I slid back into our schooldays banter.

I shook my head as I hung up the receiver at the thought of an ex-hippie, Vietnam protestor writing a weekly political journal in the Bluegrass region of Kentucky.

I grabbed my keys and headed out the door. I started learning my way around Lexington by driving the streets in hopes of seeing her car. It was a shot in the dark, but I didn't have other options. If I couldn't find Lisa, I'd head to the next address on my growing list of the Olivers' former residences.

So far, there were five former addresses that covered the last three years of their lives. I could keep busy just following those leads, but they wouldn't likely lead me to their daughter.

Cran sent any updated information weekly via *Western Union*, charging the fees to the *Summary*. We needed a break soon, or I'd have to abandon any hopes of that great story.

Near the University of Kentucky campus, I caught sight of a blue beetle turning left on Nicholasville Road. I made a quick right and kept pedal to the metal to catch up, praying no cops were around.

I still had eyes on the car at the next red light but couldn't make out the driver or the license plate, so stayed close. When the driver swung into a gas station, I drove another few feet to a parking lot and turned in, grabbed my camera and adjusted the focus.

The driver passed a bill to the service station attendant and spoke.

I couldn't make out what was said, but the voice was masculine.

Tension had tied knots in my neck and shoulders. I shrugged a couple of times and then glanced at my watch. It was past my usual time to call in. Better find a phone booth. Hamilton was not going to be happy.

Jake

Russell was already seated when I entered the diner. He stood and offered a large, bony hand. He hadn't changed much, grin a mile wide and still a walking skeleton. At least six-three, he couldn't weigh more than one-eighty-five or so. He almost resembled a proper businessman until he opened his mouth.

"Can you dig it?" He smoothed a hand over his white shirt and red paisley tie.

"Well, at least you're still wearing jeans." I pulled out a chair and settled in.

"Man's, gotta draw the line somewhere, you know?"

A waitress stopped by and took our order. I followed Russell's lead and ordered two eggs over easy with a side of bacon.

"Comes with grits, two biscuits, homemade preserves, and all the coffee you can drink," she said.

"Sounds good to me." I looked at Russell. "You look great, how have you been?"

He shook his head. "Thank you, sir. You don't look so bad yourself. Writing a travel column, huh?"

"My editor is calling it, *Jake on the Road*. Kind of a fluff piece." I gritted my teeth in a mock grimace.

"Well, don't sell yourself short. You've got talent. You can take that and turn it into a platform."

I had an inkling what he meant by platform. I had read a couple of his recent articles, so I answered with a shrug.

Breakfast arrived, looking mighty tasty, and the coffee wasn't bad. I was about to duck my head for a silent prayer when Russell spoke.

"Do you mind if I ask a blessing over the food?"

Not what I'd expected. A quick nod and bowed head camouflaged my expression but after his prayer, I had to ask, "What's up with that?"

"All your fault, man. You, and your clean lifestyle in school. You never realized it, I'm sure, but it really impressed me. I watched you."

"You watched me?"

"Hey, I did my best to tempt you."

I nodded. "Yes, you did."

"But you never gave in, not once. And you kept at me to go to those Bible studies. I finally snuck into one, toward the end of school. You weren't there, but Ralph, the leader of the group led me to the Lord. It took me a while, but I finally got my act together. Then, last year, the wife and I attended a big music festival over in Wilmore."

"*Ichthus*, really? Wait. Did you say wife?"

He set his coffee cup down. "Yes, I did. Best thing that ever happened to me." He eyed me. "You made that possible, too."

"How so?"

"She was a church girl, man. Wouldn't have given the old me a second glance."

I dug into the grits. "I have to give God the praise for that, Russell. I sure never knew my life had an effect on anyone. Not like that. Look at you now. Making a name for yourself in political circles. Planning to run for office one day?"

"No way, I'm having too much fun complaining about politicians. If I became one, I'd have to shut up."

We laid into the food after that and when our plates were clean, Russell paid the tab. I objected, but he waved it off.

"Hey, I invited you."

Out on the sidewalk, he gestured to a storefront across the street. "There's my humble daytime abode. Want to see it?"

"Sure."

The phone was ringing as we entered. Russell picked it up. "Yes, sir, I'll see you then."

He turned back to me. "Say, I was thinking. I have extra office space, why don't you set up in here while you're in the region?"

"I wouldn't be in your way?"

"No." He led me to a small office at the back. "The

desk is old, but it's usable, and you'll have a phone."

"Oh, hey, that would be great. I could reimburse you for whatever long distance calls I make."

"Sure, whatever. Are you in a hotel?"

"A former motel over on Versailles Road."

"Sure, I know it, used to be the old Thoroughbred Inn. So, they rent rooms long term now, huh?" He stepped to a desk near the front of the main office and opened a drawer. "I think I have a spare key. Yeah, here it is." He handed it over.

"I can pay rent."

He waved it off. "No way. No rent required."

After we sealed the deal with a firm handshake, I headed for the door. "Next time, I'll buy breakfast."

He gave a hearty laugh. "Anytime, man, anytime."

As I drove back to my room, I mulled over Russell's offer. It was an answer to a prayer I hadn't even prayed yet. But could I keep the Oliver story under wraps? Russell had an inquisitive nature.

The mess I'd left on the table in my room made my decision for me. In under an hour, I had the chaos organized and packed into a box ready for transport. All set for the morning, I grabbed my keys and headed out for more scouting.

I had to find Lisa.

I drove straight to the University of Kentucky campus and worked my way back. Not a Volkswagen in sight.

I headed out Old Frankfort Pike to check some of the area horse farms. An article in last week's local paper featured a particular farm that was open to personal tours by appointment.

I slowed for a tight curve and noticed a dark car bearing down on me. I picked up speed. So did the other driver.

Pisgah Pike loomed ahead. I turned and hit the gas. The dark car also turned. I gripped the wheel as my pulse sped into high gear.

My limited knowledge of the area left me in a quandary. The narrow, tree-lined road offered no way out. The other driver kept his distance, slowing almost to a stop near an ancient cemetery. After a blind curve, a lane to the right provided me with an escape. I pulled onto it, and headed for a large, black barn.

The barn seemed abandoned, so I pulled in behind it and got out to watch the road. The black vehicle crawled past. From my vantage point, I couldn't make out faces, but the passenger appeared to have a bouffant hairstyle. I leaned against the barn wall and gave my racing heart a moment to slow down.

This cat and mouse game was for the birds. I shook my head at the inane double idiom. I was a writer for goodness' sake. When I turned to go, I almost fell over at the sight of a dark horse standing beside my car, nonchalantly chewing on a tuft of grass. It stared at me, and I stared back. How had I not heard the approach of so large an animal?

A deep breath steadied my nerves. "Hello, there. Nice to meet you." I tugged at a juicy looking clump of tall grass and offered it. The animal sniffed it and me before accepting my gift.

I leaned forward to look it in the eye. "Could I trouble you to find another parking spot? Maybe you hadn't realized it, but you're blocking my door."

Out of nowhere, a voice piped up. "That ole mare doesn't talk, sir. Not a word."

I leaned to the right and peered around the horse to find a man dressed in overalls, green plaid shirt, and straw hat. I chuckled. "I really didn't expect an answer. Sorry if I'm trespassing."

The man stepped closer, lifted a bridle over the horse's head, and settled the bit in her mouth. "No bother at all. I understand. We're a ways from any facilities out here."

Wait, he thought I was . . .

Before I could counter his assumption, he offered his hand.

"Name's Sheldon. This is my land, and my wandering mare. She's like Houdini. She can get out of any enclosure. Always looking for greener pastures somewhere else."

I shook Sheldon's hand and laughed at his joke. "Nice to meet you, Sheldon. I'm Jake Bradley."

He nodded and tipped his hat. "Well, Jake Bradley, I'm going to take this sneaky horse back to her stall. Pleasure meeting you."

It had indeed been a pleasure. The short meeting with the weathered farmer had gone a long way toward settling my frayed nerves. Back on the road again, I chewed a licorice twist and formed a decent article for my next travel post. I'd leave out the suspected car chase, of course.

When I arrived at my temporary abode, I found a note taped to my door. Hamilton wanted to talk to me. Inside my room, I left a message with his secretary for a return call. Moments later, my phone rang.

"I received your first two columns. Good stuff."

No greeting, just the facts but I did notice his tone was

less gruff. "Thank you, sir."

"We need a face-to-face. When can you be here?"

I stared at the ceiling. Why? Was he going to pull the Oliver story? I cleared my throat. "I can drive over tomorrow, so how about Thursday morning?

"Eight a.m. Sounds good. See you then."

CHAPTER THIRTEEN

Jake

The scene outside the window of Hamilton's office at the *Asheville Summary* held my attention as he read my latest offering. A gray pigeon roosted on the concrete windowsill. It wasn't much but was the only thing that kept me from doing something juvenile like chewing my fingernails.

Hamilton guffawed.

I stared at him. Had he really just laughed at my article?

He dropped the paper on his desktop. "Good stuff, Bradley."

"Thank you, sir."

Elbows on his desk, he leaned forward. "Now, where

are we with the other story? Have you found the girl yet?"

"No, sir, but I'm close."

"Close isn't good enough. You need to find her, Bradley. This is dragging on too long."

"I agree. I'm making every effort—"

"Effort is costly. But these articles you're writing are stirring up interest. I like that. More importantly, the owner likes them. Keep 'em coming. Make those your first priority."

"Sir?"

He tapped his finger on my story. "The travel column, Bradley. The Oliver story may never pan out. But you're onto something with articles like this one. Readership translates to dollars in our industry."

I bowed my head as my stomach clenched. He was inches away from shutting down the Oliver story. I had no choice but to acquiesce. "Yes, sir. I'll do my best."

"What's on your mind, Jake?"

I snapped to attention. He never called me Jake.

His eyes on me, Hamilton sat back in his chair. "Spit it out."

"I was just wondering why I had to drive all the way back here for an attaboy."

A deep rumble sounded in his chest, followed by a

slow headshake. "I called you back here to relieve you of your assignment, Bradley. I figured it was a lost cause." He picked up my article and waved it in the air. "But this is pure genius. You saved your bacon with this latest piece. I'm giving you one more month. Get me something solid, or you'll be Jake on the road in North Carolina."

Hamilton pressed his intercom button.

His secretary answered, "Yes, Mr. Hamilton?"

"Greta, get a check issued for Mr. Bradley. Another month's expenses."

"Right away, sir."

I blew out a breath. *One more month.* "Thank you, sir."

Lisa

A scream woke me. At least, I thought it was a scream.

My heart raced, my breath came in jagged spurts, and I was sweating. What kind of place had I moved into? Then, I heard it again.

Now that I was awake, it had more of a metallic sound. I struggled free of my sleeping bag and crept to the window. It was early morning, barely light. Below me, someone revved a car's engine, and it made that sound again.

Ray stood beside the car. At the loud squeal, he lifted his hand and called out, "Shut it off." He crouched beside the car's window. "Fan belt's loose."

Great. If Ray worked on cars, this could be a busy place.

I backed away from the window. Lowering to my knees, I rolled up the sleeping bag and pushed it against the wall, where I could use it as a cushion. It was a multifunctional sleeping bag.

I'd only been in Lexington for a week, but it seemed much longer. On Wednesday, I'd interviewed for a clerk's job at the engineering firm and was hired on the spot. A good thing, because I didn't have a phone and didn't know when I'd be able to afford one, but it was only for the summer. If all went well, I'd be back at EKU in August.

A scratching sound at the door made me smile. Ray had warned me the cat liked to pay visits. I opened the door just wide enough for her to squeeze through. "Good morning, Jax."

I washed my face and combed my hair before returning to the kitchen to heat water for tea. I toasted a couple of slices of bread under the oven broiler, buttered them, and sat down on the sleeping bag. Jax helped me eat the toast.

After breakfast, I stood and crossed to a rickety card table I'd found at a yard sale down the street. It held the contents of the dreaded box. I picked up Mom's sweater and held it against my chest.

How could she be gone?

I folded it and laid it with a pair of Dad's jeans. There wasn't much here. A few tattered papers, Mom's purse, Dad's billfold. Tears threatened again. How long would this go on?

There seemed to be nothing of value in the box. No clues to help me locate Mom's cash stash, if it even existed. Maybe her final payment to the college had emptied it.

Could I manage to pay for spring semester and graduation? I'd have to save almost every penny I made this summer. With what I had left in my savings account in Richmond, I could probably do it.

I squeezed my eyes closed and fingered the rings I wore on the chain around my neck. I kept Dad's watch in my purse, wound it every day to keep it ticking. I'm not sure why, but it comforted me.

Sitting cross-legged on the floor, I sifted through the

papers, mostly bills marked *paid*. A letter to Dad confirmed employment at Capital Trucking.

Another slip of paper held my writing. *Best of luck in your new location. Love you!* I'd tucked that note inside a box of Mom's favorite chocolates. She'd probably finished those before she'd reached the state line.

Pain stabbed my heart at the thought of her blithely downing chocolates on the way to her death. I ran my fingers through my hair, gathered it into a ponytail, and secured it with a rubber band. What did I expect to find?

Something, anything. A clue.

Mom's purse yielded only a few items. A lipstick, a compact, a well-worn copy of *The Lord of the Rings*, and her billfold. I looked in every pocket. Funny, how little she kept in there. She didn't even carry a picture of her daughter.

Where had the money been kept?

Should I even care? Did hunting the money make me mercenary?

Picking up Dad's wallet, the emptiness returned. Though weeks had passed since the accident, I still felt numb. I'd get to a certain point and then shut down.

Forcing my fingers to move, I unfolded the wallet. A Kentucky driver's license. A couple of fifty-dollar bills I couldn't bring myself to remove. That was all.

No credit cards.

No photo of his daughter. They were all in the pink and white box.

Mom had told the patrolman they'd left to protect me. So, maybe that's why they didn't carry a single photo of me. But who were they protecting me from? And why had Mom's last request been for the nurse to send for me? Was the supposed threat over?

I sat on the sleeping bag and leaned my head against the wall as weariness threatened to overwhelm me.

STILL WATER

CHAPTER FOURTEEN

Lisa

On Monday, May 17, I drove to Addison-Allegro Engineers to report for my first day of work. I was the new kid on the block again.

"Are you familiar with the ledger card bookkeeping system?" Mrs. Withery, the middle-aged head bookkeeper, held a metal file box that no doubt contained the aforementioned cards.

Her dubious expression encouraged my rebellious streak. With a slow intake of breath, I managed to quell the inclination. "Yes, ma'am."

She didn't seem to want more information, so I stopped at that.

"Let's find you a desk." She led the way into a large

interior office filled with gray metal desks in three rows. Each work area held a lamp, a typewriter, and an adding machine. Most were already occupied, but one near the back stood empty, its green blotter-style cover awaited the stacks of files and papers the other desks enjoyed.

Phones rang and were answered. A quick scan told me that each middle desk held a phone. A soft voice spoke over the intercom. "Mr. Buckson, line one. Mr. Buckson, line one."

I concentrated on the movements of the woman in front of me as she set the box on the empty desk.

"You can sit here, next to Miss Huddleston. If you have any questions, she'll be your guide."

My gaze drifted to the right, where an attractive young woman labored over a column of figures. She had the most perfect hair I'd ever seen, a mass of tiny corkscrew curls.

"No dawdling, though," Mrs. Withery added, her eyes on Miss Huddleston.

The younger woman looked up. "No, ma'am." Her dark-eyed gaze cut to mine with an expression that barely hid humor.

I liked her already.

The air in the room seemed to clear after Mrs.

Withery's departure.

"She's not so terrible," Miss Huddleston whispered through a dazzling smile made more brilliant by the dark tones of her complexion.

I did my best to return her warmth. "Thanks, I'll keep that in mind."

After I situated myself at the desk, I opened the metal box, revealing a file of eight by ten ledger cards.

The woman in the desk behind me snickered. "Good luck. She gives that scary box to all the newbies."

I raised questioning eyes to Miss Huddleston.

She nodded. "It's true, she does. It's kind of a test. Just do your best, follow her instructions exactly, and you'll be okay."

Instructions? Panic fluttered in my chest. Had the woman given me instructions? My breath calmed as I noticed the word, *Instructions* on the first ledger card. A numerated list of twelve items. I read through it and then started the test.

An elongated tone sounded at noon.

"That's lunch break," Miss Huddleston said. "I hope you brought your lunch."

I pulled the small brown sack that contained my peanut butter sandwich and a can of soda out of my purse.

"I did."

She rose, a plastic container in one hand, and a thermos in the other, and used her hip to push her chair under the desk. "Join me for lunch?"

I nodded. "I'd love to."

"It's a beautiful day. I love to eat outside when the weather's nice." She pushed through a side door to a nicely landscaped garden where some of the other employees already occupied benches and tables.

A few more people exited after us. Their squinty-eyed expressions reminded me of groundhogs emerging from winter retreats.

"Oh, the sun is shining!" One young woman said.

I hid my smile behind a bite of sandwich. Would it hurt to add windows to those offices? An architectural engineering firm should lead the way designing comfortable workspaces.

"So, where are you from?" Miss Huddleston's question jarred me from my inward thoughts.

"I've been living in Richmond while attending EKU."

She bit into a delicious-looking roast beef sandwich. "Oh, what's your major?"

I tried not to covet her sandwich, but I couldn't keep my mouth from watering. I swallowed before answering,

"English major, business minor."

"Hah! Good thing you're minoring in business, unless you're planning to teach. Does your family live in Richmond?"

I washed down a bite with a sip of soda before shaking my head. I'd planned to keep this part of my life private, but my coworker's warmth melted through my defenses. "I don't really have any family."

Her brow furrowed. "I'm sorry. How long have you been on your own?"

"Not long."

She chewed slowly, her eyes on the well-manicured lawn in front of us.

I could almost hear the unspoken questions so obviously on her mind. I had no doubt she'd ask them at some point. In the next few minutes, I learned that she was a year older than me, one of four children, all girls, and she attended church regularly.

Three tones sounded and everyone headed back inside. What an odd place. I'd never worked anywhere so regimented.

At a quarter till five, the phone nearest me jangled. The woman who occupied that desk answered. "Yes, Mrs. Withery, I'll tell her." She looked at me. "Mrs. Withery wants to see you in her office."

"She'll want you to bring the box," Miss Huddleston whispered.

I stored the cards inside, closed it and carried it to the front where Mrs. Withery occupied a small office.

"Have a seat," she ordered.

Perched on the edge of a gold, Naugahyde chair, I watched while she thumbed through the cards. Her brow furrowed, as her lips pursed.

My heart fluttered. Had I made an error and botched the test?

She closed the box. "You followed directions exactly, Miss Oliver. You're ready to begin training. Have you any objections to being trained by Miss Huddleston?"

Objections? What was that supposed to mean? "No, ma'am." Perhaps they'd had race issues in the past, but it wouldn't bother me. How could anyone object to Miss Huddleston?

"Good. I'll see you in the morning."

Dismissed, I headed for my desk to retrieve my belongings. The elevator door opened as I passed by, and several men in business suits stepped out. These were probably the engineers, whose offices were upstairs.

One, a man of medium height, dressed in a light gray

suit and red paisley tie, stopped when he saw me.

Revulsion twisted in my midsection as his gaze crawled over my form. I turned my back and kept walking as another of Dad's quotes played in my mind.

Never trust a man who can't keep his eyes on your face, kiddo.

I wanted to stop in the ladies' room and wash my hands, but the five o'clock tone sounded. Navigating against the current of departing employees took all my concentration.

Miss Huddleston had waited for me. "I'll walk out with you."

We spoke in low tones until we were away from the building. She had warned me that too much fraternizing was discouraged. What a silly rule. Employees should enjoy working together. I gave a mental shrug. Perhaps there was a reason for the strictness.

"You drive a beetle?" Miss Huddleston stopped in front of Little Blue, sitting by itself near the edge of the already half empty parking lot.

"I do. Is that funny?"

"No, I love Volkswagens. I want a pink one."

"Hah, I've never seen a pink one, but I think it would suit you. I hope you get one someday, Miss Huddleston."

She beamed. "Please call me Starr."

I returned her smile. "That's a great name. I'm Lisa."

"Well, goodbye, Lisa." She nodded toward a tan Pontiac waiting near the front walk. "That's my ride. I'll see you in the morning." With a final wave, she strolled to the street.

About that time, several of the engineers exited the building. I got in my car and headed out before anyone noticed me. I had no desire to be ogled again.

Little Blue's fuel gauge registered empty, so on the way home from work, I stopped at a gas station and ordered a dollar's worth of gas. Even with such a small order, the young attendant still insisted on washing my windshield.

He was probably flirting with me.

As I pulled out of the station, I passed a dark blue vehicle parked near the telephone booth. A man stood inside the booth, talking on the phone. As he pushed the door open, I had the distinct feeling he was watching me.

"Gee, Dad, if your goal was to make me paranoid, you certainly succeeded."

I shook off the feeling and stepped on the gas.

CHAPTER FIFTEEN

Lisa

Overall, my first day of work had not gone badly. At least I'd been busy enough to keep my mind from wandering.

I parked my car beside the steps to my apartment and got out.

Ray stood in the garage, wiping his hands on a rag.

A short, dark haired woman with a round, pleasant face stood next to him. She tilted her head to the side when she saw me. A smile lit her eyes as she stepped nearer. "Hey there, you must be our new boarder. I'm Elaine, Ray's wife. Sorry I haven't been up there to meet you yet. My mother's been ill, so I've been in the country."

Her eastern Kentucky twang tickled my ears. "Nice to

meet you."

Ray tossed the rag aside. "How'd your first day go?"

"Good. I think it'll work out."

After a quick glance at her husband, Elaine spoke, "You had some visitors today."

Who knew I was here? "Visitors?"

A frown creased her brow. "Two guys in business suits. They seemed real put out that you weren't home."

The slump of her shoulders and slight downturn of her lips told me she'd expected more of a reaction from me. I was not sorry to disappoint. "I can't imagine who it would be." I kept my eyes averted, examined my keys, taking time to run a few possibilities through my mind. Lawyers? Insurance agents? "Did they leave their names?"

Ray leaned against the car he'd been working on the last couple of days. "Said they'd try again later, so I expect you'll see them at some point." His eyes were guarded, as though he suspected me guilty of a crime. "I thought maybe they were selling encyclopedias or something, but Elaine didn't think so."

Jax broke the tension as she wound through my ankles and then plopped down on the bottom step.

Elaine shook her head. "That's one spoiled kitty. I hope she hasn't been bothering you."

"Oh, no. I've enjoyed having her around."

"Well, you be sure and let us know if you need anything, you hear?"

"Thank you." I hurried up the steps before she could continue. I had a feeling Elaine was an energetic conversationalist.

Upstairs, with the windows thrown open to catch a breeze, I found some music on the clock radio. My gaze shifted to the front window every few seconds. Who was looking for me and why?

After changing out of my work clothes, I retrieved the shoe box from its hiding place in the back corner of the closet. Why I'd felt the need to hide it, I couldn't say. And I wasn't ready to contemplate the reasons why Mom had abandoned it.

Abandoned me.

Could she have hidden a clue inside?

I sat on my sleeping bag and removed the lid. A tangled mess of photos and memorabilia lay inside. Within a short amount of time, I had them sorted by year.

If my parents had truly left to protect me, leaving any evidence of my existence behind might've done the trick. But why didn't they tell me, or at least leave me some clue?

What was I supposed to think?

I got up and stretched. The voices downstairs had quieted. Ray and Elaine must have gone into the house for dinner. A glance out of the window told me the sun was going down. It would soon be dark. Another long night lay ahead. I really needed something to occupy my time.

Perhaps I should buy a jigsaw puzzle.

Mom and I used to work puzzles together. The memory made me smile until my stomach growled, sending me on a hunt for sustenance. I warmed up a can of chicken noodle soup before sitting back down on the floor.

While it cooled, I picked up a wallet-sized black and white photo of me as an infant wearing a frilly dress. I'd always wondered about it. Someone must have given the outfit to Mom. I couldn't see her buying something like that. Mom had owned one very plain shirtwaist dress. One. She lived in flannel shirts and jeans.

Not me. I'd always preferred dresses.

The date on the back of the photo read, *April 12, 1950*. It seemed almost as if something had been erased. I shook my head. Probably just a smudge from so much handling over the years.

So far, I'd found nothing out of the ordinary. No

hidden messages. My stomach clenched as hope faded. I picked up the bowl and ate a couple of bites before returning to my examination of the photos. Most held some sort of inscription, a date, a location, or an event.

Once the pile of photos dwindled, I noticed something else in the box. Envelopes, pressed tightly against the bottom. There were three, all in the same handwriting—Allison Pearl's—my best friend from my senior year in high school.

I determined the oldest one and set the other two aside. She had promised to write to me when I left for college, but I'd never heard from her. Checking the address she'd sent them to, I realized why. She had mailed them to a P.O. Box my parents had used at the time. Why had she done that? I had given her my dorm address before I left town.

The letters were still sealed, which further raised my curiosity. I tore one open and removed three pages.

Dear Lisa,
    I can't believe I'm writing to you at college! That's so exciting! I hope you'll have time to answer and tell me all about it so I can experience it along with you.

Oh, my. Poor Allison. How long had she waited for an answer? And all the while, I was waiting for her to write.

> *I begin classes next week at the community college. A few of our classmates were at the orientation. I suppose it won't be so bad, but nothing like the excitement of a real college. I envy you so.*

A dull ache inside increased to full-blown anxiety as I read all three letters. Poor Allison. She had never known why I hadn't answered them. The final paragraph revealed her hurt feelings.

> *I hope I haven't bothered you, writing multiple times, but you did ask me to. I'm going to believe that you're busy studying and just don't have time for a small-town nobody friend like me. I'm still glad to have known you, and happy for all the memories we shared as seniors in high school. I hope you have a wonderful life, Lisa. I wish you great success in all you do.*
> *Sincerely yours,*
> *Allison.*

There was a period after her name. I glanced at the other two letters, but no period. Maybe she had done that because it was to be the last one.

What must she think of me? I folded the letters and returned them to their envelopes, then tucked them back in the box.

We had been best friends from the first day we met. Hers was by far the tightest friendship I had known in my short life. I'd been so disappointed when I didn't hear from her, so why hadn't I written her anyway?

Dumb, Lisa, really dumb. If I had written, she would have known about the address. She would have answered and maybe, I'd still have a best friend.

Where was she now? Did she finish her two years at college? Had she married?

I bit my lip. Was it too late for me to write and tell her what had happened, or at least find out why she had used that address? But if Mom had been the one to give her the information, how would I explain that?

Sorting through more of the photos, I found the ones from my senior year of high school.

One showed Allison and me, dressed in shorts, peasant blouses, and white sneakers, sitting on Little Blue. Allison's mother had taken that one. Rick, Allison's brother, was in the next one. He had sneaked up behind us to get in the picture.

Allison's willowy figure, long, light-blond hair, and contagious laughter made her popular with all our friends. She had taken me in. Her whole family had, especially her mom, Elsie Pearl.

I picked up the photo of Allison and me all dolled up for the prom. In the last one, I stood next to Rick, my prom date. He was fourteen months older than Allison, but had been held back a year, so he graduated with us.

He'd had such a crush on me. I liked him, but not enough. I had bigger plans. I was determined that nothing would stop me from going to college at Eastern Kentucky and graduating with a teaching degree.

I laid the photos back in the box, keeping everything in order, and returned it to the closet.

Maybe I would write to Allison. Was she still living at home? The Pearls had stability. Allison's dad had grown up on that property. He would never have left it. For a moment, I wondered what that would be like.

Why had Mom kept the letters from me?

I would probably never know. My life had become a heap of unanswered questions.

CHAPTER SIXTEEN

Lisa

Voices droned in quiet conversation. Mom and Dad sharing a cup of coffee in the early morning. I snuggled inside my sleeping bag as a sense of peace enveloped me. Then I remembered Mom and Dad were gone and forced my eyes open.

Sunshine streamed in my windows, announcing the lateness of the hour. The murmuring reached me again but this time I recognized Ray's voice.

Chores beckoned. Boring, everyday things like hand washables and ironing. Work was my remedy, my go-to. Staying busy kept the ache at bay. When I had no more work, the remainder of the day stretched out in front of me like an endless wilderness.

Spying Mom's copy of *The Lord of the Rings*, I picked it up and opened to a page marked by a corner fold. She'd underlined one of her favorite quotes from Gandalf, "It is not despair, for despair is only for those who see the end beyond all doubt. We do not."

Mom never despaired, but always held to hope.

Shaking off the melancholy, I dressed to go out. I could afford a cup of coffee at my favorite café.

Trudy welcomed me with a broad smile. "Hi, Lisa. I just put on a fresh pot. Be about five more minutes."

I found a seat at the counter and glanced around. Good timing, the place was nearly empty.

Trudy returned with a steaming cup. "How've you been, hon?"

I stirred in the cream. "Not bad."

"More importantly, how's the job going?"

"Good. I haven't met your brother yet, though."

She shook her head. "You probably won't see him. He's on the survey crew. Summer's their busy season. They're out at dawn and sometimes work till dark." She frowned at me. "Have you been eating? I know how it is with you college kids. Have you even gotten a paycheck yet?"

It was kind of nice, having someone worry about me.

"I have food." I took mental inventory of my cupboard. Four cans of soup I had gotten on clearance. A pack of crackers, and half a jar of peanut butter. I would need another loaf of bread.

Trudy slid a small plate in front of me.

Pecan pie, my favorite, but I couldn't afford it. I shook my head. "No, thank you."

She scrunched her nose and whispered. "You can pay me next time. Just don't tell anyone, or I'll charge you double." She grinned and winked.

The door opened and closed. I looked up, but didn't recognize the man who walked in. Not that I expected to, I hadn't been here that long. Story of my life.

Trudy nodded to the man. "Have a seat anywhere you like, sir. I'll be right there." She turned toward me. "Be right back, sweetie."

The pie and coffee kept me busy as she waited on the newcomer. I tried not to but couldn't help checking him out. He was maybe mid-twenties, with dark, shoulder-length hair that he kept tucking behind his ear. His light blue tee shirt fit well over rippling muscles.

Heat rose in my cheeks as I swiveled back around. Sometimes, I hated being so observant. Dad's training kept me on constant high alert. In some cases, like when I noticed rippling muscles, it could trip me up.

Trudy turned in an order. "B.L.T., no mayo, sticks on the side."

I smiled at her name for French fries. Mom had also called them sticks.

Trudy filled a glass with ice and cola and delivered it to the man. "Your order will be right up."

"No problem." He spoke in a low voice, but his accent sounded vaguely familiar.

I sneaked another peek at him. This time, he caught me. I turned back and helped myself to another bite of pie.

Trudy topped off my coffee. "Careful there, sugar. You almost fell off the stool." She cackled and shook her head.

"Order's up," the cook said.

Trudy grabbed the sandwich and fries and hurried toward the man's table.

I kept my head down until she returned, already planning my retreat and how to get out of here without her embarrassing me. I liked her, but she was a little too forward at times. I waited as long as I dared, and then counted out correct change for the coffee and a tip. "The pie was delicious, Trudy, thanks. It's been a while."

"Take care of yourself, hon. Stop in when you can."

I headed for the door. Though I never turned to look, I felt the man's gaze on me. Not thinking about him took all my concentration as I got in my car and drove away. But I did notice the dark blue Camaro parked in front of the café. There weren't any other cars out there, so it had to be his. I had seen it recently, but where?

Didn't matter. I would never see him again.

Jake

Lisa left, and I couldn't follow. Too obvious. I had made a discovery, though—she was friendly with the waitress, so was probably a regular at the *Bluebird*.

After the last bite of my sandwich, I wiped my fingers on a napkin and retrieved pad and pen from my pocket. Bluebird Café, Nicholasville Road area. Three miles from the University of Kentucky campus. I paused and clicked my pen. Apartments and rooms to let should abound in this area.

The waitress headed my way. "How was your meal, hon?"

Flashing a smile, I noted her name tag. "Best BLT around, Trudy. Thank you."

She tore off a ticket and laid it on the table. "You are most welcome. I haven't seen you in here before. Are you passing through, or new in town?"

"I'm here for a few weeks. I write a travel column for a newspaper in Asheville, North Carolina." Aware of an Asheville, Kentucky, I added the state for clarification.

"Oh, wonderful. There's so much to see and do in our beautiful state, especially here in the Bluegrass. You here for the races?"

"Yes, ma'am. Keeneland, and all the horse farms in the area are a definite draw, as well as the natural wonders and historical landmarks. Fodder for my articles."

She smiled and nodded. "Too bad you can't feature some articles in our local paper. I would love to read them."

"Syndication, that's every reporter's dream."

"Refill on your soda?"

"No, thank you, I've had enough."

She was about to turn away, but I needed information, so I just blurted it out, "Hey, that girl you were talking to—the one that just left—she looks familiar. I think I may have seen her before, but I can't remember where."

Trudy's eyes narrowed.

Bad sign.

She stepped away to retrieve a tip from a neighboring table and stuffed it into her apron pocket. "Did you attend college around here? Maybe that's where you've seen her."

"I was on the EKU campus a couple of weeks ago."

"Could be that's where she's from. I only just met her a few days ago. She's a little forlorn, so I give her extra attention." Still no smile as she moved away.

Trudy was loyal. I had to admire that. I left a dollar on the table, picked up the ticket and headed to the register where an older lady with a well-rounded figure punched in the amount.

I handed over the cash. "I'm on a business trip, so I'll need a receipt, please."

She printed off a copy and handed it to me, along with my change and a warm smile. "You come back and see us."

"Oh, I will."

Outside, I rubbed the back of my neck, yearning for a smoke. In the car, I reached for a licorice twist. It was a bit stale, but I didn't care.

Fully fortified, I cruised the surrounding neighborhoods, paying close attention to apartment complexes.

STILL WATER

A baby-blue bug sat in front of a long row of apartments, but a closer look revealed a white racing stripe running along its side. There was no luggage rack on top, and the license plate was not hers, so I continued on my way.

I didn't waste my time in the newer subdivisions. Brick ranch houses seemed an unlikely fit. I continued toward Lexington's cityscape where shady streets held small, white cracker box-style homes. Detached garages might mean apartment space, which made sense in a college town.

A few blocks nearer to town, the houses were older and larger, with spacious lawns. Many of them had garages. I slowed my pace.

Half an hour later, I was ready to concede defeat when a flash of light blue caught my eye. I hit the brakes, shifted into reverse, and then stopped. There it was—a little blue Volkswagen, complete with luggage rack—in the drive beside a two-story garage. An outside staircase led to a second-story apartment.

Lisa

Jax meowed loudly.

"What's the matter, girl? Are you hungry?"

There was only enough milk in the fridge for one more bowl of cereal.

Jax rubbed her head against my ankle and meowed, making the decision an easy one. After pouring some into a bowl for her and replacing the carton, I kicked off my shoes and turned on the radio. It was warm inside, so I opened the windows.

An odd growling sound drew my attention back to the cat. Her eyes riveted on the closed door, she emitted a second low growl and swished her tail.

What in the world? I stepped closer and then almost fell over the frightened cat when someone rapped hard enough to rattle the door.

I stood still a moment to catch my breath, and then put Dad's door opening lesson to good use. Blocking it with my body, I opened the door just far enough to peek out. The two men on my landing would have no trouble pushing past me if they so desired.

The nearest man spoke with authority. "Lisa Oliver?"

"Yes?"

He held up a badge. "FBI, Miss Oliver."

STILL WATER

CHAPTER SEVENTEEN

Jake

The street I was on connected to a main thoroughfare, so I jotted down the address and then found a place to turn around.

I needed to get a closer look at the VW. Short of knocking on the door, turning around was the only way I could get close enough to see the license plate.

On my approach, I slowed to a crawl, and took in my surroundings. Kids played basketball in their driveway next door. Two younger children rode their bikes on the sidewalk.

When the boys in the neighbor's drive stopped to stare, I pulled over and parked on the opposite side of the street.

They soon lost interest.

I turned my attention to the house with the garage apartment and did a doubletake. A dark blue sedan had blocked my view of the Volkswagen.

Was someone visiting the house, or the apartment?

I picked up my camera, removed the lens cap and focused. I couldn't see any movement in the house. Peering through the branches of a large tree, I made out the figures of two suit-clad men on the steps leading up to the garage apartment. My heart sank into my stomach when I recognized Agent Farrow.

I was too late.

Lisa

I stepped back enough to open the door wider. The first man spoke.

"Miss Oliver, I'm Agent Zach Farrow, and this is Agent Matthew Evers."

Agent Evers didn't look much older than me. His brief smile and pleasant demeanor reassured me, but why were they here?

Agent Farrow pocketed his badge and leveled his gaze

at me. "May we come in?"

I hesitated, mainly because my unfurnished apartment provided little opportunity for entertaining, not to mention my shoeless feet. "Um, yes, I guess." I stepped aside. "I'm not really settled in yet."

"That's all right," Agent Farrow said. "This is not a social call."

The two entered.

Heat rose into my cheeks as they surveyed the apartment. After switching off the radio I moved to the card table and gestured toward the folding chairs. "May I offer you something to drink, uh, water, or—"

"No, thank you." Agent Farrow laid a folder on the table and eased onto the chair as though he expected it to collapse.

Agent Evers took up a position near the door. Did he expect me to make a run for it?

I sat across from Agent Farrow, tucked my bare feet beneath the chair, and folded my hands in my lap as Dad's admonitions played in my mind.

Be vigilant. Always be aware of your exits and map out an escape plan. That way, you have the upper hand and any attempt at surprise is defeated.

Agent Zach Farrow had unremarkable features, short

brown hair, and brown eyes. A slight frown creased his brow. "Miss Oliver, I'm investigating the accident that took the lives of your parents."

My jaw went slack. Why would they need to investigate an accident? "Investigating?"

He nodded. "We received a tip from a reliable source that what happened that night may not have been an accident. With that in mind, I'd like to ask you some questions."

I shifted in my seat. "Questions?"

He nodded as he opened the folder and removed a paper filled with typewritten questions, each preceded by a number. "This won't take long. You are Lisa Renee Oliver?"

I glanced up at Evers, who nodded and smiled.

"Yes, sir."

Agent Farrow clicked his pen. "You are a student at Eastern Kentucky University?"

I nodded.

"And you were there when you received news of your parents' car accident?"

"Yes, sir." The shock of the phone call rushed over me again.

He eyed me. One brow arched. "When had you last

spoken with your parents?" His pen waited for my reply.

"The day before. They took me out to dinner before they left for Asheville." Dad had scratched his head a lot, something he did when nervous or anxious.

Agent Farrow made a note and then raised his eyes to mine. "And then?"

"They took me back to my dorm and then they left." Mom had clung to me in a tighter hug than she usually gave. I didn't believe in premonitions, but having to go back through everything, memories resurfaced. Things I hadn't noticed that night.

"What time was that?"

For some weird reason, I glanced at the clock radio on the kitchen counter. "It was seven-thirty, I think."

"To your knowledge, did they plan to drive all the way to Asheville that night, or did they plan to stop along the way?"

I shook my head. "Dad preferred to drive at night. Less traffic."

He jotted that down. "So, that had been his habit?"

I nodded. "He was a truck driver. He knew the roads."

He sat back. His eyes narrowed. "He knew the roads."

"Yes. I mean, he'd traveled all over, and he'd already been to North Carolina when he interviewed for the job."

I suppressed a chill at the memory of Dad flying around blind curves in the dark.

"Another truck driving job?"

Something about his expression told me he already knew the answer. "No, it was different. He was going to retire from driving. I think he called it a scheduling job."

He nodded. "Did they give any indication of anxiety, or worry over the move?"

I hesitated, remembering Dad's expression when they left. In light of what I now knew, his parting expression haunted me. "Not really."

"Miss Oliver?"

I watched Agent Farrow. Should I tell him what the patrolman said, or did he already know that too? Most likely, they had already interviewed those who spent the last moments with my parents.

I drew a breath. "At the time, they seemed normal."

He lowered his gaze as he fingered his pen. "Normal." He clicked the pen closed and then open again. "I believe you met the patrolman who was at the scene of the accident?"

So, he had talked to the cop. I nodded. "He told me what my mother said. Her . . . uh, last words."

"Her last words? What exactly did she say, or rather,

what did the patrolman tell you she said?"

Why did he insist on asking questions unless he thought I knew something, which I did not? A quick glance at Agent Evers told me he knew all the facts, too. I could imagine them discussing my involvement in detail. Were they trying to catch me in a lie, or collusion, or . . . maybe I'd read too many detective novels?

I looked down at my hands. "She told the patrolman they left to protect me."

"Were you surprised by that, or were you aware of a problem?"

I scoffed. "I have no idea why she would say that. I was shocked. My parents were very reserved. They never talked about things. Except—"

He leaned back, his eyes on me. "Except what?"

My first opinion of him had shifted. His overall countenance was unremarkable, but his eyes revealed clear thinking. He read me like a book.

I moved my hands to the table, palms down. "Dad was careful. He was protective and proactive. He taught me to always be wary."

I cast a glance around the small apartment. One way in, one way out. Not so good. Dad wouldn't like it.

Aware of danger, aware of my surroundings at all

times.

Agent Farrow tilted his head sideways. "I see. Tell me about your dad. He was a truck driver, so I suppose he was on the road a lot, away from home. Did he have any friends? Did anyone come around?"

I kept my eyes on the table in front of me. "Well, we never lived anywhere very long."

"So, no friends that you know of?"

I shook my head. "My parents didn't even associate with the neighbors. They kept to themselves."

"Did they ever give you any reason or understanding of their actions?"

I crossed my arms over my chest. The chair creaked as I leaned back. "No. They were introverts. They seemed content to be by themselves."

"What about you, Miss Oliver, did you keep to yourself?"

He probably knew every friend I'd ever had from birth until now. "I always had friends, at school and in the neighborhood."

"And that was all right with your parents? They were okay with that?"

I averted my eyes. No, they had never really been okay with that. If they'd had their preference, I would have been an introvert just like them. I kept my voice low as I distanced myself from my emotions. "They tolerated my friends at times, but no one was welcome in our home. I went to their homes or played in their yards. When we left a place, we left my friends behind."

He sat forward. "You didn't keep up with any of your friends, even after you were older?"

I shook my head to indicate a negative answer. I couldn't trust my voice not to break. I couldn't help thinking of Allison Pearl and how hurt I'd been when she didn't write, and all the time, it was . . . I sucked in a breath.

More than anything, I wanted Agent Farrow to change the subject. This was supposed to be about my parents, wasn't it?

After what seemed like hours as Agent Farrow wrote extensive notes on countless sheets of paper, he set his pen down and eyed me. "I think we've bothered you long enough, Miss Oliver." He gathered the papers, shuffled them into a neat stack, and tucked it into the folder. Then he pushed away from the rickety little table and stood. "Will you be returning to college this fall?"

I stood, nearly knocking my chair over in the process.

Before I could react, Agent Evers caught the chair and

set it aside.

I nodded my thanks, while trying to ignore the heat rising in my cheeks. "Yes, it's my senior year."

Agent Evers opened the door and stood aside for Agent Farrow.

As I followed them out the door, I remembered something. "Agent Farrow, may I ask you a question?"

The two men stopped and looked back at me.

Agent Farrow nodded.

"My mother said they left to protect me. Am I in danger?"

CHAPTER EIGHTEEN

Jake

I hung up after a long but fruitful conversation with Cran, leaned back, and rubbed my neck. What had I gotten myself into?

"Morning, J.B."

I looked up to find Russell headed my way. I gave him a nod.

The checkerboard tile floor and a stainless-steel counter running along the back wall of the interior hinted of a former life as a bar or café. I would guess a bar, because of the occasional whiff of stale cigarette smoke and an earthier scent that reminded me of hops.

His footsteps echoed across the floor until he halted at the front corner of the desk. "You're in early. By your expression, I'd guess you just got bad news."

I sat forward, shaking my head. "Not bad really, just worrisome."

"Bummer. Need to talk about it?"

"Naw." I picked up my pencil and tapped it on the papers in front of me. "I need to think it through first. Digest it."

He stepped to the window and looked out. After a moment, he turned and faced me. "I understand. Maybe see which direction to take on your story?"

I nodded. "Something like that." I leaned back, rolling the pencil between my thumb and forefinger. "Hey, I really appreciate you letting me camp out here for a few days."

"No problem at all, buddy. Stay as long as you like. I know you'd do the same for me."

As he sauntered away, I scanned my notes, adding comments where I needed more clarification. Then I picked up the phone and dialed my editor's number. I left a message for a return call, so Russell wouldn't get charged for long distance.

I worked on my notes until the call back came fifteen minutes later. Not bad. "Hello?"

"What have you got for me?"

Once upon a time, Hamilton's gruff tone had unnerved me. Not anymore. I chuckled. "I may have bitten off more than I can chew."

"Well, you better fill me in."

"Along with the latest list of former addresses, my source was able to get a copy of a police report that stated, 'Forensics found three bullet holes in the driver's side door, but only one bullet, which was deeply embedded in the dash near the glove compartment.' Of course, there were no bullet wounds in either of the Olivers, so it is possible those were warning shots. Maybe the shooter was trying to scare Oliver. This is consistent with the conversation I overheard that day at the scene of the accident, I don't believe they were trying to kill the Olivers, probably just trying to stop them."

Several seconds of silence passed before the boss responded.

"You need to get on this right away."

"My thinking exactly."

He gave a loud sigh. I could imagine his expression as he worked through the information. "Have you interviewed the daughter yet?"

"No, sir. I was waiting for this report."

A loud smack sounded over the phone—his hand

hitting the desktop?

"You need to talk to her. Before the Feds do, if possible."

I closed my eyes. "They were there yesterday."

"What? You know where she is, and you haven't gotten an interview?" He huffed. "You know this is going to make it ten times harder. She'll think twice about talking to you."

I wanted to snap back but instead took a deep breath. "They beat me to her place by minutes, sir."

He muttered something unintelligible. "Do whatever it takes to fix this, then." Click.

He hung up on me. *Uncool.*

I returned the receiver to its cradle. This was a setback, that was all. I would find a way. I had a reputation to uphold, a job to hang onto. And the memory of that girl's haunted expression still filled my mind.

I slept in on Sunday. Since the weather was nice, I took a drive, making a point of slowing down as I passed Lisa Oliver's apartment. Her car was there, but I couldn't make myself stop. What would I say to her? *Hi there, I've been looking for you?*

Sounded like something she might hear at a frat party.

No, this would require some delicate strategy, and I needed to clear my mind.

Some of the most scenic countryside in the nation lay within minutes of downtown Lexington. Especially this time of year. Miles of low stone walls bordered the narrow, winding roads. The leaves of ancient maples formed a thick canopy above me. Many of the long, private drives were bounded by rows of daylilies in full bloom. Things my readers would appreciate.

When I found a place to pull over, I got out of the car to stretch my legs. I sat on a grassy knoll and watched a couple of colts frolicking in the paddock. My line of vision rose to the blue sky where a hawk made silent circles overhead.

A country boy through and through, I broke off a blade of tall grass to chew on while I ruminated the pickle I was in. My brain worked better in the open with birdsong and the trill of insects for a soundtrack.

In my mind, I had a couple of options. Honesty. Tell her who I was—Jake Bradley—working on a story about the tragic accident that killed your folks. *And oh yes, you could also be in danger.*

Or I could hang out at the café, hoping to meet her. But what if she didn't return there for a week or so? I didn't have that kind of time.

Then there was the possibility that Agent Farrow had warned her about me after the way he had strongly cautioned me to steer clear of this case.

Back in my car, I grabbed a licorice twist. The cravings came less and less these days. I found myself with some extra change in my pocket as well since I wasn't buying smokes all the time.

Within minutes, I was again driving down the street where Lisa Oliver lived, paying close attention to my surroundings. The warm summer day brought the kids out to play.

As I passed the house, I noticed a small handmade sign in the front yard, "Cars Repaired."

"Yes!" I thumped the steering wheel with the palm of my hand.

A basketball bounced into the street right in front of me, and I slammed on the brakes.

A lanky kid retrieved the ball and held up his hand to thank me for stopping.

Good thing I'd been cruising along slowly. At the end

of the street, I made a left and headed back to my temporary home while my mind filled with possibilities. I might have found my way in, but the timing needed to be perfect.

STILL WATER

CHAPTER NINETEEN

Lisa

I was not in any immediate danger. Agent Farrow had assured me of it, but I was not convinced. Two days had passed, and I still couldn't stop thinking about it.

If whoever is responsible for your parents' death had wanted to do you harm, you would have known it already, he had gone on to say.

Quite possibly, I would've been dead already. Such were my thoughts, but his words made sense.

He had also warned me against talking to anyone about what we had discussed. "The less people know about this, the better for our investigation."

"No immediate danger," I whispered. My head and heart were not in sync, however. Not at all. I glanced around my apartment. One way in, one way out. Not the best setup.

"Map it out, girl," Dad's voice echoed in my mind. We'd been at a dime store, and he'd fired off the questions so fast, I'd had trouble following. "First things first. What's your escape route—where's the nearest exit—alternate exits?"

"Uh, uh, front door, back door?" I hadn't been able to see any windows that opened. Had I gotten it right? More than anything else, I sought his approval.

"Not good enough, kid. Walk around, check it out." Dad had jerked his head toward the back of the store. "I'll be right here."

I had only been ten years old, but I'd known from the tone of his voice there was no use in objecting or complaining. I'd walked the aisles. Two clerks and a handful of shoppers. All the windows were high except the front ones, but those didn't open. A narrow passageway at the back was marked, "Employees Only." At the end of the passageway a door had a lighted exit sign above it.

"Can I help you?" The stern face of the older woman had frozen me to the spot. She glared at me as though I'd been casing the joint.

"No, ma'am, I was just waiting for my dad. Sorry, I

guess I got distracted." I had looked around and found Dad standing at the cash register. "There he is."

I had run to his side, where I remained, constantly checking over my shoulder to the place where the older lady stood, watching me like a hawk.

Dad shook his head at me. "Never let them see your fear, kid. They'll use it like a weapon. Don't let anybody intimidate you. Stand your ground."

Stand my ground. I glanced around my apartment. Dad would be concerned. I focused on the room again. I needed to prepare myself for an emergency.

The drop below the windows was a little too high. I would end up with broken bones. Ditto on the bathroom window, except there was a large tree outside that one. I pushed the window open and leaned forward. The nearest limb was close enough, but it would be difficult.

I glanced around the tiny bathroom. I could lock the door or maybe wedge a chair against the knob. That would give me another minute or so to get out. But what if there was more than one intruder? The other one could be waiting on the ground.

A tremor ran through me. Wow, my mind went to the scariest possibilities.

I leaned against the wall and drew in a couple of deep

breaths. My throat felt thick, and my heart raced. I closed my eyes. I had to get hold of myself. It was stupid to panic. Stupid.

No one was after me. If they had been, I would have known it already. I had been vigilant. I'd watched the rearview mirror when I made the trip back from North Carolina. There had been times, I was the only car on the road. I had not been followed.

However, I was easy enough to find. The FBI certainly hadn't had any trouble.

The reality that I was fully alone for the first time ever settled on me again like a straitjacket. I had been raised to be independent and self-sufficient, so, why was I freaking out over it now?

I opened the closet door. Barely two feet by three feet, there was no room for me to hide. The overhead shelf was—wait—what was that? A sliver of light shone above the shelf.

Armed with a flashlight, I grabbed one of the folding chairs and wedged the back of it against the door jamb so I could stand on it without breaking my neck. I shone the light on the closet's ceiling, following the edges from corner to corner. Could it be?

I jumped down and used the broom handle to press

against the ceiling. It moved.

"Aha, a trap door into the attic."

I would need a stepladder to access it. I should be able to find an inexpensive one somewhere. I added it to my list before replacing the chair. The closet door creaked when I pushed it closed. Needed oil, something I already had in the emergency kit in my car. My mind raced ahead. If there was attic space, there must be a window or a vent up there or there wouldn't be light coming through the cracks. The possibility eased my anxiety.

I slipped my shoes on and headed outside. Near the front of Ray's house, I turned and looked back toward the garage, shading my eyes with my hand. There it was—a round attic vent near the peak of the roof overhang.

I was still looking at it when I heard a car pull in behind me. I glanced over my shoulder as the dark blue vehicle approached, its engine thrumming. I turned around. My jaw went slack as the man I'd seen in the café got out of the vehicle and strode a little too close for my comfort, forcing me to take a backward step.

He spoke through an amused smile, blue eyes sparkling. "Hello. Sorry if I startled you."

"Uh, hello." What was he doing here, looming over me like that? Up close, he seemed much taller than when

I'd seen him at a distance. And he smelled like licorice.

He ran his fingers through his dark hair. I caught a glimmer of what looked like a class ring. "I'm looking for the guy who works on cars."

"Oh, that's Ray." I glanced toward the closed garage. "He's probably in the house." I gestured toward the door.

The guy nodded but still faced me. "Have we met? You look familiar."

Why were my hands shaking? I folded them together. "At the *Bluebird Café*, I think. I mean, we didn't actually meet but I think I saw you there."

His gorgeous eyes never strayed from my face. He was polite as he spoke with a definite Tennessee drawl. "Yeah, that's it. Small world." He stuck out his hand. "I'm Jake Bradley."

I hesitated, but only a moment and then lifted my chin as I offered my hand. "I'm Lisa Oliver."

Jake

"I'm Lisa Oliver." She spoke in a whisper-soft voice.

Our handshake, if you could call it that, lasted but a second. The girl was as skittish as an untrained colt.

Or maybe not. I shifted my stance as her warm brown eyes searched mine. A brain scan would have been less intrusive.

Behind us, a screen door opened and shut. I turned to see a short, middle-aged man standing on the back steps.

Lisa stepped forward. "Ray, this is Jake Bradley. He's looking for you." She glanced at me.

Ray started forward. I met him halfway. "I saw your sign out front and wondered if you could help me. Not today, of course, since it's Sunday." I turned to look behind me, hoping to find Lisa. She'd taken a seat on the steps beside the garage. A gray cat lay sprawled next to her.

Ray's eyes widened when he caught sight of my car. He licked his lips. "Camaro. Super Sport. Sixty-eight or sixty-nine?"

I nodded. "Sixty-eight." My eyes wandered back to the girl and the cat.

Ray cleared his throat. "What's the problem?"

I tore my eyes away from the girl and the cat and walked toward my car. "She's running a little rough. Plugs, or maybe ignition points off a little?" I raised the hood and then stepped around and leaned inside to start the engine. I'd made a few adjustments of my own before driving over. Nothing that would hurt the engine, just enough to convince Ray I needed help.

He ducked under the hood and cocked an ear. "Sounds like timing. Or could be plugs. Maybe both." He stood and looked at me. "She's a beauty. I can take a look at it in the morning, if you can bring it back by."

I shut off the engine. "Sure, tomorrow's fine."

"Any time after seven a.m. I'll be out here in the garage."

"All right if I drop it off and come back for it later in the day, maybe around five-thirty?" I shot another quick glance toward the girl. She should be home from work by then.

Ray nodded. "Sure thing. I'll see you in the morning."

As Ray returned to the house, I looked at Lisa. "Thanks for your help, Miss Oliver."

She smiled and waved. "No problem."

I got in the car and backed slowly out of the drive, careful of where I was going, but keeping her in my sights as well. I would be happy to walk a couple of miles or more, just to see her again.

Where had that thought come from? She was the subject of a story. An article. And an important one. One that I needed to keep my head in.

Not some bundle of crazy emotions.

STILL WATER

CHAPTER TWENTY

Lisa

I lay awake, startling at every noise. Why was I suddenly so afraid? Was it that guy—Jake? He had passed my preliminary inspection, but a girl couldn't be too careful. Especially a girl on her own.

My thoughts wandered from my new acquaintance— that's all he was—to the attic space above me. This morning, I had borrowed a step ladder from Ray's wife and found the attic hot and draped with cobwebs. Someone had placed boards to provide a platform, probably used in the past for storage. I could sit on that and wait out an intruder. Just me and the spiders. Creepy, but better than the alternative.

On the way back down, it occurred to me that I could

put the box of photographs up there. I was not sure why it seemed important, other than the fact that they connected me to life, and I did not want to lose that. Shelby would've called it odd behavior, and she would probably be right.

I'd almost drifted off to sleep when someone gunned their engine nearby. Desperate, I got up and moved my sleeping bag until it abutted the door. This was another one of Dad's tricks.

We were in a motor inn along a lonely highway. I was twelve.

"Crawl into bed with your mother," Dad had told me. Then he'd dragged my sleeping bag to the door of our room and lay down.

I had asked Mom about it the next morning while Dad showered.

She'd shrugged as if it was nothing of great importance. "His way of guarding the door."

I'd responded with bugged eyes. Guarding against what? My vivid imagination must have kicked into overdrive.

She had put her arm around my shoulders. "There's nothing to be afraid of, kid. It's just this remote area. He worries that someone may see us as easy prey, break in and steal all our stuff." She'd laughed out loud. "They'd be disappointed, wouldn't they?"

I had nodded, but my insides never quite let go of the fear.

The same feeling washed over me as I listened to the night sounds of the neighborhood, guarding my own door. Fear still kept a stranglehold on my life.

Starr waved when I entered the office. As I settled in, she smiled at me.

"Mama sent enough lunch for the both of us if you'd like to share. I told her you usually eat peanut butter sandwiches."

"I won't turn that down, thanks." I had already sampled Mrs. Huddleston's cooking. The peanut butter sandwich in my purse would keep until supper.

She darted a glance toward the door when someone entered. That signaled the end of our conversation, but I was sure looking forward to lunch.

I almost groaned aloud at the name on the cover page of a file left on my desktop. Tim Sanders, the guy who had ogled me in the hall. I breathed out a sigh. So far, I had managed to avoid any contact with him. It had not been easy. Now, I'd be working directly for him.

I thumbed through the file. Right away, I had questions. Was he testing me, or was this his way of making contact?

I pulled a job list from my drawer and studied it. Much of the information should be there. I filled in the missing items and double-checked it. My next step was to coordinate with the project manager.

With an inner cringe, I glanced at the clock. It was barely ten.

The phone on the middle desk rang. Miss Barlow picked it up. "Yes? Yes, sir, right away." She hung up the phone and looked at me. "Mr. Sanders wants you in his office to discuss the Tri-Lex project."

I straightened the file, grabbed a legal pad and pen, and pushed away from my desk. As an afterthought, I donned Dad's watch, pushing it up on my forearm.

Starr's gaze bored into me, but I could not bring myself to look at her.

As I passed, she whispered, "Be careful."

I took the stairs. Even here, windows provided lovely views of trees and grass and flowers. I could almost enjoy the trek except for the meeting with Mr. Creepy.

This was only my second time upstairs. All the engineers had titles and private offices with floor-to-ceiling windows, plush carpeting, and tasteful furnishings in muted tones. What would it be like to work in a place like that? I had never dared to dream of it.

My eyes straight ahead, I walked the central hallway to the office at the back and knocked on the door. Mr. Sanders didn't have a secretary.

"Come in."

At the sound of his voice, my hand recoiled. I pulled in a quick breath and opened the door. "You wanted to see me?"

He looked me up and down. "Sit, Miss Oliver."

I sat, crossing my legs at the ankles, tucked beneath my chair.

His lips quirked. He hadn't missed the move. "Let's see what you've done so far."

I handed him the project file.

He watched me for a moment before opening the folder. "A smile wouldn't hurt, Miss Oliver. I'm sure it would brighten your outlook, as well."

A small smile was all I could manage.

He scanned the forms. "Looks good, except for the project information. You are obviously working with an outdated project list. Ask Mrs. Withery for a new one." His jaw tightened as he closed the folder and laid it on his desk. Those bloodshot eyes rolled over me again. "You know, Miss Oliver, I can make your life a lot easier here."

My stomach lurched as I forced myself to meet his gaze.

"You just have to be nice." He handed me the file. "A woman with your looks," he paused to lick his lips, "and obvious intelligence could be doing so much better than the dungeon, Miss Oliver."

The dungeon. That's what the engineers called the clerical offices. I reached for the file. "Thank you, Mr. Sanders. I'll keep that in mind."

Before I could stand and turn, he had moved to the doorway. How had he gotten there so fast?

Creepy smile firmly in place, he watched me pass. I was pretty sure he watched me walk all the way down that hall.

I went directly to the ladies' room and stared at my reflection in the mirror. "There will always be bullies. You just have to recognize them and learn how to deal with them," I said aloud. Then I took a deep breath and blew it out.

After washing my hands for the third time, I opened the door and headed toward the front office. No amount of soap could cleanse away the stain of being leered at. I wanted no part in anything that man could offer. I just had to get through these next few weeks until time to return to school. My nerves calmed at the thought. School and a crowded dorm sounded so good right now.

I tapped on Mrs. Withery's open door.

She sat back. "Hello, Miss Oliver. What can I do for you?"

"Mr. Sanders said I needed an up-to-date project list."

Her expression changed so slightly, I almost missed it. "Close the door and have a seat, Miss Oliver."

I sat and settled the file in my lap.

She peered at me over the top of her glasses. "So, you've met with Mr. Sanders."

It wasn't a question. I nodded in agreement.

"Is that the project file?"

I nodded again.

"May I see it?"

I handed it over.

She thumbed through the contents and then returned

to the first sheet and ran a finger down the page. She raised her eyes to mine. "I see nothing wrong with this project information. In fact, you have done an excellent job on these forms, Miss Oliver."

"Thank you."

"Did Mr. Sanders say anything else to you?"

My gaze dropped to my hands.

"You're not his usual prey, Miss Oliver."

I looked up. "Excuse me?"

She sniffed and shook her head. "He's one of those men who seeks to take advantage of weak-minded young women. You are not one of those. I'm surprised he chose to hit on you."

Her smile reassured me.

Until it flattened into irony. "Did he say he could make your life easier, free you from the dungeon?"

Relief rushed in as an invisible weight lifted off my shoulders. She knew. "He did."

"You're smart enough to know he can do neither of those things. You are a good employee, Miss Oliver. I will hate to lose you, but a college degree is your ticket to a brighter future. I hope you'll make the best of it." She handed me the file.

"I intend to try." I stood. "So, I assume there's no

updated project list?"

"There is not. We update the project lists weekly and make sure everyone has their copy. My guess is, he sent you to my office, thinking I would berate you for assuming we had not done our jobs properly. But I'm on to him. While I have no authority over what he does, I can stand in his way."

I had no doubt she would. As I left her office, the lunch bell sounded. At least Starr and I would have something to talk about as we enjoyed that delicious meal.

STILL WATER

CHAPTER TWENTY-ONE

Jake

At five-thirty sharp, I walked up Ray's drive to reclaim my car. He had parked it near the back porch. The VW was not in its usual spot, which meant Lisa was not yet home. I found Ray in the garage, checking the tire pressure on a white Pontiac LeMans. The tantalizing mixture of axle grease and motor oil, typical smells of a garage, always sent me back to the days when my dad tinkered on his various automobiles.

Ray stood and smoothed the front of a once-white cotton work shirt that barely covered his belt. "Punctual. I like that." He nodded toward the Camaro. "I got her all tuned up and ready for you. I took her for a test drive. That's a bad car, man. You're a lucky dude."

I grinned at his attempt at youthful jargon. Renting to college students seemed to have given him a decent handle on it. "Thanks, I try to take good care of it."

"She's a beaut." He shook his head and then walked over to his worktable. "I cleaned the plugs and adjusted the timing, checked all the fluid levels and tire pressure. No more problems."

"What's the damage?"

He chuckled. "I oughta pay you for the privilege. But I reckon that wouldn't be good business." He sucked his teeth. "Twenty-five oughta do her." He looked past me as another vehicle pulled into the drive.

I didn't have to look. I recognized the sound. Lisa was home.

I tugged out my wallet and offered him a ten and a twenty. "Keep the change."

He folded the bills and tucked them into his breast pocket. "Don't mind if I do. Keys are in the car." He raised a hand to salute Lisa. "Afternoon, Missy." Then he turned back to me. "You have a good rest of the day, now, you hear?"

Lisa held a brown grocery sack in either arm. She pushed the car door closed with her hip and dropped her keys.

Her grimace made me smile. I rushed to grab the keys and then reached for one of the bags. "Here, let me help you."

Her cheeks flushed a rosy hue, but she released the nearest sack. I trailed along behind her as she climbed the wooden steps to her door.

After unlocking it, she set the bag inside. When she turned to take the one I held, I got a glimpse of a lot of empty space inside the apartment. Had she no furniture?

I got the feeling she didn't want me to see, so I stepped back down and leaned against the railing.

Still holding the grocery bag, she gave me a shy smile. "Thanks for the help."

I spoke before she had time to disappear inside. "Hey, can I call you sometime? Maybe we could meet at the Bluebird for dinner or something." She was shaking her head before I finished speaking, but I was determined to finish.

"I don't have a phone."

Not an outright no. I took that as a good sign. "Okay, how about Friday around six?"

She bit her lip, sending all kinds of sensations through me. "Six?"

I nodded, encouraging her with a smile.

She took a breath and slowly released it. "I guess it would be all right." She gave me a sideways glance. "Just dinner though. I have to study."

I pushed away from the railing. "Study? Are you in summer school?"

She shook her head. "No. Preparation for a tough class this fall."

"Just dinner, then." I was a tad disappointed, but an hour or two was better than nothing. "See you at the Bluebird on Friday."

I started to leave but turned back, taking the ever-present ink pen from my breast pocket. "In case something comes up, here's my number." I jotted my phone number on the front of the grocery sack. "If I'm not there, you can leave a message."

She smiled the first real smile I had seen. It was pretty amazing. As I turned away, I glanced toward the clouds scudding by overhead and whispered, "Please don't let anything happen to postpone Friday night."

Would God answer my prayer? I hoped so because I sure wanted to spend more time with her.

Lisa

Friday was usually a little on the slow side at work since many of the engineers took off a couple hours early. At least that had been my three-week experience. Not so this time. The heavy workload kept everyone hopping until well after four. I was glad for the busyness since it helped keep my mind occupied. I did not want to think about dinner with Jake. Even the thought sent nervous twitches through me.

I finished the last project file and handed it off to Starr. She checked it and added it to the stack.

"Can you believe this?" She laid her hand on top of the pile of folders. "I think we may have broken a record."

Beside me, Miss Barlow spoke. "Summer's always busy, but this year does seem more active."

I glanced at the clock. Ten more minutes. I spent the rest of the time organizing my desk for Monday. When everyone began to leave, I grabbed my purse and followed.

Starr waited outside the employee exit, an impish grin on her face. She fell into step beside me. "I hope you enjoy your not-a-date."

I chuckled. "That's funny. I hope so, too."

"Are you always so careful with prospective

boyfriends?"

"I'm alone in the world. I have to be careful." The weight of that statement was beginning to lighten just a bit.

She eyed me for a moment. "I know what you mean but you're not really alone. You know that, right? If you ever need anything, I'm here for you."

Fighting back tears, I concentrated on my feet as we descended three steps to the walkway. "I appreciate that."

"And Mama, too. She wants you to come to dinner one night so she can fatten you up," she finished with a giggle.

"I'd love that."

She tilted her head to the side and smiled. "Of course, she'll preach at you, too. Mama does that."

"I don't mind." Once upon a time, I would have. But friendship meant more to me than differing opinions and beliefs.

After Starr set off across the parking lot to catch her ride, I paused and dug around in my purse for my keys. Why do they always fall to the bottom?

When I looked up, Mr. Sanders leaned against the driver's side door of my car, arms crossed over his chest.

He had abandoned his jacket and tie and rolled the sleeves of his white shirt to the elbows.

Fighting the inclination to run after Starr, I looked him square in the eyes. "Can I help you with something?"

Usually, a smile improves a person's looks, but when this man grinned, the opposite was true.

I found my keys but fumbled and lost them again. *Drat.*

For once, his gaze stayed on my face. Still creepy. He tilted his head forward. "My meeting went late, or I would have called you upstairs. Have you thought about my offer?"

I stood still, as I finally managed to hook a finger in the ring of my keychain. "Your offer?"

He shook his head. "Miss Oliver—may I call you Lisa?"

No! I held my tongue as he ignored my frown.

He arched his brow. "Yes, my offer to help you move up in the company. Your work shows real promise. I think you have the talent to rise quickly in the ranks. With my help, of course. It's something I like to do, help folks achieve their potential."

Folks. Right. I ignored a familiar thrumming sound somewhere close by. I had heard that noise before, but my attention needed to stay front and center. "So, I've heard."

Mr. Sanders straightened. "What did you say?"

Why was this happening when I was in a rush to get somewhere? I glanced at Dad's watch. I wouldn't have time to go home first. Impatient, I jangled my keys and looked at him. "I've heard you're always willing to help young ladies. I thank you, but I'm not interested."

He stepped so close, I felt his breath on my cheek. "You know it works both ways. I can help you, or I can make your job a misery."

In my peripheral vision, I noticed someone step into view, but I could not take my eyes away from this man who was threatening me. I wanted to hurt him, in the worst way. Dad had taught me several basic self-defense moves.

As I contemplated which to use, the new arrival spoke in a deep voice, "I don't know you, sir, but that sounded an awful lot like a threat. You wouldn't be threatening my girl, would you?"

CHAPTER TWENTY-TWO

Lisa

His girl? I knew that voice and now the thrumming sound I'd heard made sense, but how had he ended up here? When had I told him where I worked?

Mr. Sanders took a backward step as his startled gaze flitted between me and the man who was now standing beside me. A man whose presence sent a strange sensation pulsing through my body.

I darted a quick look at Jake. He seemed to tower over Mr. Sanders.

As the two men sized one another up, neither said a word.

After what seemed like a full minute, Mr. Sanders glowered at me and then spoke to both of us, "I wasn't threatening her. I was just explaining how things work around here." He eyed me. "How things are supposed to work."

Before I could answer or even react, a steady arm rested at my waist. I wanted to resist but at the same time, I wanted to comply.

Jake looked at me. "I'll bet you were."

I met his gaze. Though I kind of liked that spark of anger in his eyes, I hoped it was a temporary thing. I really didn't want to get involved with an overly protective guy. I'd seen that happen to a friend, and I was not interested.

Jake released me but stayed close. As Mr. Sanders stalked off without a rebuttal, Jake ducked his head. "You ready to go?"

Not trusting my voice, I nodded.

"I'll be right behind you."

I nodded again, unlocked my door and got in. Relief washed over me and with it, a bevy of questions. How had Jake happened along at just the right time? Had I mentioned where I worked? I didn't think so.

I shifted into second and accelerated. I could have handled it myself. I know I could have.

Maybe.

I had to admit, though, this would make it easier.

While waiting for a light to turn green, I smiled. A fake boyfriend might discourage Sanders. As long as my fake boyfriend knew the proper boundaries.

My stomach churned as I shifted into third. Sanders had said he could make work miserable. But he had looked terrified of Jake.

How had that man suddenly appeared at my workplace? The question wouldn't let me go.

By the time I parked in the gravel parking lot at the Bluebird, I had an agenda. If he couldn't answer my questions to my satisfaction, I would leave.

Jake pulled up beside me.

I hooked my purse strap over my shoulder. Crossed arms resting at my waist, I waited on the sidewalk as he strode toward me looking all manly and in the moment. I didn't know him well enough to interpret the expression on his face, so I forged ahead. "How did you know where I work?"

Jake

As soon as I saw her standing there with her arms crossed, I knew I was in trouble. Of course, I had considered it earlier, before I pulled into that parking lot where she worked. How would I explain my presence?

I drew a breath. "I didn't. I was across the street at the library. I just happened to see you. Who was that guy?" I turned the tables on her. That worked sometimes.

"So, you just thought you'd swoop in like a knight in shining armor?"

Huh? Not the answer I had expected. I scratched my head. Me with no words. Even more surprising. "Um, no. I mean, I didn't really plan that move. I just reacted."

A smile quirked her lips.

Wow. Was she pulling my chain?

"However you came to be there at that exact moment, I'm grateful. Thank you." She relaxed her arms and hooked a thumb in her purse strap.

I heaved a sigh of relief. "Are we still having dinner? I hope so because I'm starving. All this charging around on a white horse makes a guy hungry." I pulled the door open and stood aside for her to pass.

She gave a cute little chuckle. "We're here. We might as well eat."

We found a corner booth and sat down. A waitress brought us menus and water. We both ordered colas.

Lisa scanned the room. "I guess Trudy doesn't work

evenings."

"Yeah. I mean no, I've never seen her here in the evening." I scanned the menu and glanced back at her. "The special tonight is meatloaf. It's good, I've had it a couple of times."

She nodded.

When the waitress returned, Lisa ordered a cheeseburger. I ordered one, too.

Lisa folded her arms on the table. "I appreciate you saying what you did. I hope he'll leave me alone now."

"I hope so, too. If not, just let me know. You have my number." I grinned and stirred my drink with the straw.

She sipped her cola. "I noticed your license plate. You're from North Carolina?"

Observant and blunt. I liked it. "I guess you'd say I'm based in North Carolina. I write a travel column, so I'm on the road a lot." Sounded good. I had practiced it several times.

"A writer? But you're not from there are you? You don't really have the accent."

"You know the accent?" I bit my lip. *Don't get in too deep.* If she found out who I really was and what I was doing here, this whole thing could blow up. I really didn't want that to happen.

She tucked a strand of hair behind her right ear. "I have friends in Asheville."

"Hey, small world. That's where I'm based. My column is in the Sunday magazine."

The waitress returned with our food.

Perfect time to change the subject. I carefully arranged my burger before picking it up. "So, are you from Kentucky, or . . ."

She finished a bite and washed it down with a sip of cola. "Mostly. My parents moved around a lot. My three years at Eastern . . . well, this is the longest I've been anywhere."

I nodded. "Have you seen much of the area? It's really beautiful."

Something like melancholy passed over her expression. She shook her head. "I've been busy—you know—studying, working."

Serious student, not a party girl. "Are you going to be a teacher?"

She thought for a moment. "I started out that way. That was the main reason I chose Eastern. Now, I don't really know. Things have changed."

After another bite of the burger, I used my napkin to clean my fingers. "There's no rush, believe me. It'll come to you."

"Did you always know you wanted to be a writer?"

"Nope. I just kind of fell into it, I guess you'd say. When I was in the service, I was assigned to a job that required writing." I grinned at her. "I've always had a lot to say, my friends would tell you that."

Her smile intrigued me. It was appealing, but it never quite made it to her eyes. I wanted to stare into those warm, brown eyes and try to figure her out, but she was still a bit skittish. The last thing I wanted to do was scare her off. I had already picked up on her distrust of men. I needed more time to get to know her better.

"Do you like your job at the engineering firm?"

She pressed her lips together and fiddled with her napkin. "Not especially. It's a paycheck." She sat back. "I thought it might be interesting."

"But it wasn't."

She sighed. "There's a lot of red tape. Mostly filling out government forms and checking statistics."

"I can see where that would be boring. So, it's just a summer job."

She nibbled at a fry. "Yes. I'm happy to have it. It pays well. And I have a friend there, who sits near me. Her name is Starr, which is a perfect name for her. She's beautiful, and funny." When she spoke of Starr, her countenance changed. A smile lit her eyes.

"I'm glad you have a friend."

"She calls herself the token." she glanced around and then gave a soft laugh. "Starr claims she is the company's attempt at racial balance."

I had to grab my napkin to keep from spewing what I'd just put in my mouth.

Lisa laughed. "She has a great attitude about things."

"Sounds like you've gotten to know her well."

She thought for a moment, as though mulling it over. "In a very short time, I know. I've only been in Lexington since school let out."

The waitress refilled our drinks and moved away.

This would be a good time for me to broach the subject of her family. The question had been flitting around my mind throughout the meal, seeking a good place to land.

I was still planning what to say, when Lisa spoke. "Tell me about your travels. What have you seen in the area?"

My horse story brought a smile to her lips. I mentioned a few of the other places I'd visited as I drove into Kentucky.

When the waitress arrived with the check, I stopped

talking and looked at Lisa.

She glanced at the large wristwatch on her arm. I had noticed it before but didn't dare ask about it. It appeared to be a man's watch. She fiddled with her purse. Though she hadn't said a word, body language spoke volumes.

After I paid the bill, we strolled outside. It was still early, but I sensed she wanted to go. I tossed some ideas around for a second date, something safe and unassuming. "Thank you for having dinner with me. Food seems to taste better when you share it with someone."

She nodded and walked slowly toward her car. "You're right, it does. I enjoyed it. Thank you for inviting me."

Hands in my pockets, I stepped closer. "Well, I am sort of your boyfriend. We should at least go to dinner occasionally." I offered my most engaging grin.

She laughed outright. Beside her car, she hesitated, her eyes on me.

I shrugged. "I would say I'll call you, but . . ."

She gave me a melancholy smile. "I know, I have no phone."

I rubbed my neck. "I have an interview with a trainer in the morning over at *Keeneland*. Have you ever been there?"

She shook her head. "I've only seen it from the road. It was really packed last week."

"Yeah, the summer meet was going on. It'll still be crowded tomorrow, but my interview is early. I thought about going for a drive later in the day if you're interested."

She frowned and chewed her lip. I could almost hear the wheels turning. Would she, or wouldn't she?

After several moments, she darted a look at me. "Could I get a raincheck? My Saturdays are pretty busy."

The muscles tightened in my neck. Was she giving me a polite brush-off?

She looked down at her feet and then back at me. "I'm a little behind on my laundry. Boring stuff like that."

The tension drained from my shoulders as I nodded. "How about we come back here for dinner next Friday?"

She rolled her lips inward, the way a little girl did in attempt to restrain a smile. I liked it.

"All right. Shall we meet here, same time?"

I nodded. "It's a date." From behind the wheel of my car, I watched her back around and leave while all kinds of warning bells sounded in my head. I was only supposed to get information, I wasn't supposed to fall for her. But the more I got to know her, the more I realized this girl was unlike any I'd met before.

And that could spell disaster if she stumbled onto my real purpose for being here.

STILL WATER

CHAPTER TWENTY-THREE

Lisa

I liked Jake. A lot. But Dad's constant warnings wouldn't die. I could not seem to quiet them.

"Best not to trust anyone," he would say. "You're going to want to, but those boys, they'll say and do most anything to get you to do whatever they want. Believe me, I know."

Thinking about and replaying our time together, I remembered a certain reticence in Jake's clear, blue eyes. Had I imagined it?

Could I trust him or not?

I had only ever dated a few guys and never with any serious intentions. Something inside me always held back. Dad's admonitions had given me the strength to get past numerous ill-intended beaus in my first three years of college. After a while, they stayed away.

One of the few guys I had befriended told me my dad had poisoned me against men. I had laughed it off but now I wondered if it was true.

I removed a load of wet clothes from the washer at the laundromat and dumped it into my basket. Elaine, Ray's wife, had given me permission to use her clotheslines, so I didn't have to wait for a dryer to open up. I would save money, too.

Lugging the wet clothes to the car, I had to laugh at myself. I was not poor. I earned a decent salary, and my savings account back in Richmond held a tidy sum. But I could not spend it. *Skinflint.* That had been Mom's pet name for me.

I fired up the engine and headed toward home.

Frugality was not a bad thing. That savings account balance would allow me to attend my senior year of college without having to work. I would have all the time I needed to study and hold onto that four-point-O average I'd gained.

With the usual Saturday afternoon golden oldies playing on the radio, I sat on my rolled-up sleeping bag to share a grilled cheese sandwich with Jax. My tiny living quarters shone with a high gleam, everything in its place. Clothes were laundered and hanging in the closet or folded in my bag.

Thoughts of Jake had hounded my progress all day. He was a journalist who wrote about the places he visited. That's all. Would he respect my privacy?

I leaned back against the wall as dread curled its way around my heart, tempting me to fear. It was closely followed by a phrase from the Tobeys' latest letter, *Perfect love casts out fear.*" The Tobeys were always encouraging me with Scripture.

I couldn't deny the usefulness of those verses. I'd carefully copied each one into the final pages of my journal. Whenever I felt afraid, which seemed more frequent of late, I would read them and meditate on them. They never failed to comfort me.

What would my parents think? Me, meditating on the Word of God?

Jax curled up on my lap, and I began to stroke her silky fur. "Do you believe in God, Jax?"

The cat eyed me, then sank into a contented purr.

Do you believe this? Mr. Tobey's words at the graveside service still haunted me. Sometimes I woke with the words on my tongue.

Jax turned her belly up and yawned. I reached for my textbook, intending to study. I'd only read a couple of paragraphs when I heard voices outside.

The cat jumped up and headed for the door.

I opened it and followed Jax out onto the landing.

Ray and Elaine had guests, and they had brought food.

Jax wandered down the drive, probably hoping for another snack.

Back inside, I picked up my textbook, and when I did, a note fell out. Starr's handwriting stirred a memory. Earlier this week, she had invited me to a concert at a coffeehouse in downtown Lexington, near the college campus. I had given my usual negative response, so she'd written the address on a slip of paper and handed it to me.

The paper falling out at that moment might have been a sign. Maybe I should attend the concert. Of course, it would be religious. That thought didn't really discourage me, though. I looked at the note again and read the words, "Cup o' Grace Coffeehouse, 7 pm."

I stuffed it in my purse and then stepped to the closet. What did one wear to a coffeehouse concert?

I heard the music before I got out of the car. Loud. This should be good.

Starr sat at a table near the front. A young man sat beside her, and another girl sat across from him. I was poised to sneak back out the door when Starr sighted me and waved, indicating an empty chair at the table.

Moments later, I slid into the seat. During a pause in the music, Starr introduced me to her friends.

"This is Judah."

Judah waved.

"And this is our friend, Beth."

Beth nodded. "Nice to meet you, Lisa. We've heard so much about you."

I aimed a questioning look at Starr.

She laughed. "All good, girl, all good."

After the band played a couple more songs, a young man stepped to the microphone. The applause told me everyone knew who he was. "Thank you," he said. "It's great to see such a large turnout tonight."

To my right, the door opened. Evening sunlight streamed in, making it difficult to see the two who had entered. I kept my eyes glued on them as they slipped into place along the back wall.

My gaze drifted around the room, noting the location

of the Exit signs.

As the speaker began to talk about the love of Jesus, I tried to tune back in, but I kept a wary eye roving the crowd. One couldn't be too careful.

"Lisa?"

I started at the sound of Starr's voice.

"Would you like a refill?"

I had not noticed the young woman waiting beside me, a pitcher poised to refill my soda. I tried to laugh it off. "Sure."

Starr leaned forward. "You're drifting again. What's up?"

I shook my head. "I'm okay."

"Really?" She grasped my hand.

I gave her a shrug and half a smile.

"You don't like the music?" Judah asked.

With as pleasant a look as I could muster, I nodded. "Oh, yes, I love it."

Beth leaned forward. "Do you know Jesus?"

Startled, I sat back in my chair. Do I know him? "Not personally." I thought it was a cute answer, but the exchange of looks between my tablemates planted a seed of doubt in my mind until Starr laughed out loud.

She looked at her friends. "She's joking, guys." Starr

shook her head at me. "She seems so serious, and then she comes out with something like that. So funny."

Judah smiled. "So, you are a believer?"

"I believe in God. I do. I … I believe." I'd known it for some time, but I had never actually confessed it. The answer to the question Mr. Tobey had asked at my parents' grave was yes, I do believe. I was not sure when it started, or why, but it seemed I always had.

As the speaker announced the second band, the door opened again, and a couple of men left. Were they the same ones who had entered late?

I was tempted to follow them. I glanced at Dad's watch. Maybe I shouldn't stay out too late.

When my tablemates laughed, I scanned their faces. I was not sure Judah and Beth were convinced that I was a believer. My distraction probably added to their doubt.

The concert over, I followed them out, taking in the surrounding area. Darkness and unfamiliarity added to my unease. There were streetlights everywhere, but darkness bloomed beyond their feeble glow. I'd almost prefer no light at all, so my eyes could adjust and see farther away.

Starr hooked elbows with me. "Where are you parked? We'll walk with you."

I had to admit their presence helped lift my anxiety.

At the car, Starr gave me a hug. "I'm so glad you came out tonight."

The heartfelt hug dissolved the last of my reserve. I had needed to be here tonight. "I am too."

Judah shook my hand. "It was nice to meet you, Lisa."

Beth followed with something similar but by then my mind was wandering again.

I waved as I pulled away from the curb.

What would they say about me after I was gone, if they spoke of me at all? I watched them in my rearview mirror as they cavorted their way down the sidewalk.

I wanted friends. I craved the kind of relationship Starr enjoyed with those two. Yet friendship like that always seemed beyond my reach.

CHAPTER TWENTY-FOUR

Jake

Back at *The Guardian*, I penciled in a tentative schedule for the week, hoping I could convince Hamilton I had enough to go on to keep me here. Was I stretching his patience beyond the breaking point?

I still mulled that over when Russell's shout sounded from somewhere in the front office.

"Jake, Hamilton's on the phone."

I punched the blinking button and picked up the receiver. "Good morning, sir."

"Good morning to you, Bradley. I hope you have good news for me."

"I did manage a preliminary interview with Miss Oliver." This wasn't confession time. I was not sure how he'd react to the date I'd enjoyed with Lisa.

"Preliminary?"

"She's super skittish. I'm being careful."

He actually laughed. "That's not like you. You usually leave them bawling. Under different circumstances, I'd pull you back in, but we've stumbled on the goose that laid the golden eggs."

What? I dropped the pencil. "Excuse me?"

"That little travel piece of yours is taking off, Bradley. I've had two requests for syndication this week."

"What? Really? Where?"

"Raleigh and Charlotte. Oh, and I've just been handed another one—Knoxville."

I jumped up and almost dropped the receiver. Syndication? I punched the air with my fist. It wasn't the Pulitzer, but it was a regular job with a real paycheck and maybe something even better—respect.

"Uh, Bradley, you still there?"

Oh, yeah, Hamilton. "That's great news, boss. So, what does that mean, exactly? Do I need to widen my travels beyond the Bluegrass state?"

"Not just yet. Stay close to the girl and see what you can find out. Send me a tentative list of sights in the area. You still haven't visited that big cave. The wife's been bugging me to send you there."

The big cave. I could easily knock that one out this week and be back in plenty of time for Friday's date.

After Hamilton hung up, I held onto the receiver for a minute. I wanted to share my news with someone, but all my friends and family were long distance. The one person I really wanted to share it with didn't have a phone. Besides, she was at work. That gestapo she worked for regulated personal calls.

I dashed into the front room to find Russell. Man was he going to be jealous.

Lisa

"Morning, Lisa Lou." Starr grinned as I settled in.

I stifled a groan at the sight of a blue folder smack in the middle of my desk. Not a great way to start the week.

"It's like a boomerang," Starr whispered.

I opened the file to reveal more red ink than I had imagined possible. I wanted to toss the thing in the trash bin.

My neighbor gave me a sad smile. "Someone has it in for you."

Mrs. Withery's entrance brought silence. She hovered around the room for a few minutes and issued orders.

I'd been working for about half an hour when she called me to her office. I was halfway expecting to find Mr. Sanders waiting to lodge a complaint against me. Instead, my gaze lit on a familiar, gray-suited man.

Agent Farrow.

I swallowed and attempted a smile.

A concerned look on her face, Mrs. Withery excused herself and closed the door behind her.

Agent Farrow indicated the chair opposite him. "Please have a seat. I won't take much of your time. Mrs. Withery informed me that you are quite busy this morning."

The Naugahyde squelched as I settled. "Um, yes, I am."

An elbow on each arm of his chair, he steepled his fingers. "I would have called but you don't have a phone and I was uncertain whether you are allowed to receive personal calls on the job."

I shook my head. "They prefer emergency calls only." I gazed at him. A visit may have garnered more attention than a phone call. Would that result in a black mark on my record? I cleared my throat. "How can I help you?"

"We have made an official change to the case involving your parents and issued a warrant against two men alleged to be involved."

I swallowed, then nodded.

He sat forward. "Two days ago, they were sighted in this area."

Prickles started at the back of my neck. "H...here? I thought you said I wasn't in danger?"

He took a breath. "We're not sure you are. It could be coincidence. Or they could be retracing your father's steps. We think they may be searching for something."

I pressed my palm against the locket hidden beneath my blouse. "Like what?"

His gaze penetrated mine. "I'm not sure. Are you aware of anything your father may have hidden? Did he give you anything that night before they left?"

I pushed harder against the locket and shook my head. "No. They never had much of anything. What they did possess was packed into their car. Everything they owned."

His eyes held mine as the seconds ticked by on Mrs. Withery's wall clock.

"What about their personal effects? Did you find anything unusual?"

"I was told most everything washed away in that flooded river. Other than a few articles of clothing and their wallets—which were nearly empty by the way—there was nothing much left."

"You examined the wallets?" His gaze lit on my wristwatch. Dad's wristwatch.

"The wallets h...held their driver's licenses and a little cash. Nothing of interest to anyone." I removed the wristwatch. "This was Dad's."

He took the watch and turned it over. "Do you mind if I take this? I'll return it to you after it's been fully examined."

I swallowed. "Okay." What could be hidden inside a wristwatch? I pressed against the locket again.

He dropped the watch into a briefcase beside his chair before turning back to me. "I will repeat that I don't believe you to be in any danger, Miss Oliver. However, it would be prudent to be careful. Stay aware of your surroundings."

I bit my lip. My dad had trained me for this.

He stood, his briefcase in hand. "Do you still have my card?"

I rose. "Yes."

He removed a folded paper from a pocket inside his

jacket and handed it to me.

The two photos on the paper were similar to photos I had seen on the bulletin board of a post office.

"If you see these men, get to a safe place and call me at once. If you can't reach me, call the police."

A chill ran through me, but I was not about to let Agent Farrow see my fear. I nodded. "I will."

With his hand on the doorknob, he paused. "I sincerely hope I don't hear from you."

I forced my lips into a smile. "Me too."

Mrs. Withery stood outside the door, her eyes on me as Agent Farrow walked away. "I hope all is well, Miss Oliver." She indicated that I should go back inside her office. She followed me and closed the door.

I couldn't read her expression. Concern? Disapproval? A combination of both? I gripped the paper Farrow had given me and then laid it on her desk.

Seated in her chair, she lifted the reading glasses that hung from a chain around her neck and settled them in place. She frowned at the paper. "Perhaps you should explain."

I perched on the edge of the chair Agent Farrow had just occupied. "My parents died under questionable circumstances, Mrs. Withery. The FBI has ascertained that it was not an accident and believe those two men may have been involved."

She gazed at me. "I see. So, this agent was just bringing you up to speed? Is that it?"

I nodded. "I'm sorry, Mrs. Withery. I don't have a phone at home. He couldn't get hold of me."

"It seems a letter would have sufficed." She pushed the paper toward me. "Unless they have reason to believe you are in some sort of danger. Are you?"

I shook my head. "They don't believe so. He was just warning me of the possibility. It seems those men have been sighted in the area."

She shifted in her chair. "I'm afraid I will have to report this incident, Miss Oliver. Even the slightest possibility of scandal must be avoided in a business like this one." She sighed. "I would suggest you return to your desk and try to put this out of your mind. I think you have quite enough to deal with at present."

So, she was aware of the markup on my desk. I made my way back and tucked the paper into my purse. Knowing that several pairs of eyes watched me, I put a smile in place and went to work.

CHAPTER TWENTY-FIVE

Lisa

The garage door yawned wide as I pulled up the drive. Ray was hard at work. He had two vehicles inside the building and another waiting in the side yard. Business was booming.

I was nearly halfway to my door when he called to me. "Miss Lisa?"

I descended the steps and stood in the doorway.

He grabbed a rag and wiped his hands. "There you are. Just wanted to let you know, we'll be gone over the weekend. Going to the lake. Leaving on Friday and probably won't return until Tuesday."

I nodded. "Okay."

"You can keep an eye on things for us. Not that you

need to. By now, you know what a quiet neighborhood this is. We look out for one another around here."

I had noticed that. "I hope you enjoy your getaway."

"Oh, we will. Brother-in-law has a cabin on Lake Cumberland. It's beautiful there. He's got a boat, too. We go fishing and water skiing. Have all sorts of fun." He stuffed the filthy rag into his back pocket. "Any-who, the wife's going to leave you a couple cans of cat food. She didn't figure you'd mind feeding that vagabond." He finished with a grin.

I laughed. "No, I don't mind. She's no bother at all."

"Okay then, well, I just wanted you to know we'd be away."

"Thanks."

Upstairs, I raised the windows and turned on the fan, a recent purchase to help me sleep at night. Kentucky summers were nearly as hot and muggy as the ones farther south.

Turning to the closet, I opened the door and tugged at the cardboard box that held the few things my parents had left behind. I couldn't stop thinking about Agent Farrow's question, "Are you aware of anything your father may have hidden?"

I removed the contents and made a thorough

inspection of each article. I found nothing. As I folded the clothes and bent to place them in the box, the locket dangled free of my blouse. It was the last thing I'd received from my parents. I pressed the latch to open it and gazed at the small black and white faces of my parents.

"What is this all about?" I clicked the locket closed and tucked it back into my blouse. If only I could talk to them one more time. I had so many questions I needed to ask.

After returning that box to the closet, I stood on a chair, and lifted the attic door. Air drafted past me as I grasped the little shoebox that mostly held my mementos and brought it down.

Dad's wallet still held the two fifties and little else. I even tested the creases for something hidden between the layers. A rolled-up strip of paper fell out and drifted to the floor. I picked it up.

With my fingers, I spread out the flattened roll, about a quarter inch wide and nearly six inches long. A black design in the corner reminded me of a legal certificate of some sort. It looked like the top half of "US." Maybe an emblem? The decorative border had a smeared stamp.

I held it under the light. An ink blob followed by . . . *ificate of Identification.*

Certificate? There was also a handwritten cursive Z, a period, and a six-digit number—224505.

I sat back. Was it something to do with his driving?

My stomach growled. Out of habit I checked my wrist, now empty. Agent Farrow had Dad's watch. I rolled the strip of paper again and sat for a moment, thinking. If Dad had kept this, it may be something important. I tucked it back into his wallet.

I stood and walked to the kitchen sink where I washed my hands. It was too hot to cook, so I made a tuna fish sandwich for supper. Jax enjoyed licking the empty can while I ate. After sifting through all the photos and replacing everything in the shoebox, I opened my journal and recorded Farrow's conversation to the best of my ability. Then I read it through and committed it to memory.

That night, I made my bed in front of the door again.

Each morning, the blue file had found its way back to my desk. Mr. Sanders had ripped apart my neatly typewritten proposal with so much red, I could barely make it out.

"Add this."

"Delete that."

"I didn't tell you to make that change, put it back."

Starr sent me an empathetic glance. "Just take it one change at a time," she whispered.

One at a time. Right. The first round of edits had taken me all day.

On Friday, I could no longer hide my dismay. I lowered my head to the desktop and groaned aloud.

"About time you showed some gumption, Oliver."

I looked at the woman seated across from me.

She shook her head. "No one else would put up with it that long. I would have gone to Withery's office midweek."

I barely heard her whisper, but she was almost immediately shushed by another woman down the line.

They didn't want trouble, especially on a Friday, and I didn't need another black mark in my file. I was contemplating a fake illness when the phone on the middle desk rang.

The woman seated next to me answered it. "Yes, Mrs. Withery." Her eyes on me, she hung up. "Withery wants you in her office and take your work with you."

As I passed by, Starr cupped her hands together in a

prayerful pose.

Mrs. Withery reached for the file as soon as I entered her office. "Sit, please."

After a quick glance through the folder, she tossed it aside. "Mr. Sanders has lodged an official complaint against you, Miss Oliver. He says your numerous errors have delayed this project, costing the company time and money."

I blinked. I had no words.

"Of course, I am aware of the circumstances. I've made my report and it has been duly noted. However . . ."

Whatever it was Mrs. Withery had been about to say, she must have thought better of it. Instead, she jotted something on a note and handed it to me. "I've recommended you be sent home early today and docked a half-day's pay."

The note repeated what she had told me and added that today's infarction was the second warning. A third would result in termination.

I opened my mouth to object and then closed it.

Mrs. Withery gave a curt laugh. "Yes, I know it's not fair, but it will appease the gentlemen, Miss Oliver. This is what we must do." She lowered her voice. "In this office, it is all about politics, preening feathers and taking the blame. I'll do my best to smooth this over, but I can't promise anything."

I breathed deep and exhaled. "And if you can't . . . smooth it over?"

"I'll write you a fine letter of recommendation. I'm afraid it's the best I can do."

Determined not to cry or to show any other negative emotion, I rose and left Mrs. Withery's office.

Already being in hot water, I felt no inclination to abide by silly rules. When I reached my desk, I put my things away and picked up my purse. With a smile, I looked around. "I'm taking the afternoon off. See you on Monday."

This was one time I could care less whether anyone was watching my retreat.

Anger roiled in the pit of my stomach. I slammed the gears and almost burnt rubber pulling out of the parking lot. This was beyond unbelievable. How did those women work in such a biased atmosphere? Those good ole boys needed a set-down.

"Wish you were here to advise me now, Dad." At a

red light, I drew in a long, slow breath and exhaled. My heart was racing, and I needed to calm down. I tended to internalize my angst, and that was not a good thing. A few deep breaths helped.

"Every minute you remain angry, you give up sixty seconds of peace of mind." I repeated Ralph Waldo Emerson's quote like a mantra until I felt my calm return.

With a few hours to kill before my second date with Jake, I stopped in at a dress shop I'd been eying. Maybe a little shopping would raise my spirits. I hadn't bought a single article of clothing since last summer.

The shop was a bit pricey, but I found a chic little poppy-colored sundress on sale and paid for it before I had the chance to talk myself out of it.

When I arrived home, Ray and Elaine were packing their car. She waved and then called out, "I set a couple cans of cat food on the landing along with today's mail."

I nodded. "Thank you."

"That silly cat would be just fine on her own, but I figured you wouldn't mind."

"That's right. I'm happy to. Have fun."

I set the mail on the counter and draped the dress over the back of a chair. Squeezing my eyelids shut, I shook my head to clear my mind. "Snap out of it."

What was that silly song Mom used to sing called "Pick Yourself Up?" Something about cleaning up and making a fresh start. The words wouldn't quite come to mind. I opened the windows and turned on the radio.

I certainly didn't want to go out to dinner with this hanging over my head. I had to believe it would all work out. I only needed that job a few more weeks and then, good riddance.

Half an hour later, I heard car doors slam and then the engine's roar. Ray and Elaine were leaving.

What would it be like to spend a few days at a lake, enjoying life? I'd camped out before, but never for pleasure, always on the way somewhere.

It seemed so quiet after they had gone. I smoothed out the dress and hung it in the open doorway to freshen. Then I sat on the top step outside my apartment to read a couple of chapters of a book I had picked up at the library earlier in the week.

When I heard the deep thrum of an engine, I jumped up. It sounded like Jake's car, but we had planned to meet at the Bluebird again. It must have been a passerby. I stood on the landing another moment before I reached for my dress. I couldn't see anyone out there but had the uncanny feeling I was being watched.

STILL WATER

CHAPTER TWENTY-SIX

Jake

I gave a satisfied sigh as I dropped the Mammoth Cave article in the mailbox.

I couldn't say why this one had been so difficult to write. I enjoyed every moment of the excursion and took copious notes. By the time I sat down to type up the article, I was back in Lexington and distracted.

Big time distracted. Thoughts of Lisa and the information I so desperately needed filled every idle moment these days.

I pulled out of the post office and headed toward Clay's Mill Road. I just needed to see that little blue bug and know she was all right. Cruising past the architectural firm, I scanned the parking area.

It wasn't there. I pulled into the library, turned around, and passed by again, but still didn't see the VW. Was she sick? Had she taken a day off?

At the stop sign, I rubbed my jaw and wondered what to do next. I could swing by her apartment, see if the car was in the drive. If so, I could stop in and make sure she was all right.

Her car was in the drive. Okay, she had gotten home early. That was the most likely explanation. She had my number and would call if there was a problem.

I headed back to my place. As I turned left into the parking area, I noticed a dark car following. I shook my head when the driver rolled down his window. Agent Farrow. I'd been caught red-handed.

Outside my car, I stuck my hands in my pockets and put on my best how-do-you-do face. "Well, look who it is."

He got out and leaned against the vehicle. Without his suit jacket on, he looked almost human. "I was just about to say the same thing. I thought you'd left town."

I chuckled. "So, you knew I was here?"

He crossed his arms over his chest. "I read your column every week."

"Oh, you're a fan. Come to get my autograph?"

He lit a cigarette. "Maybe later. Right now, we need

to chat." He took a long draw and blew it out.

I wanted to breathe the secondhand smoke and enjoy it. Instead, I pulled a licorice twist from my breast pocket, broke off a bite, and stuck it in my mouth. "I thought that's what we were doing."

His eyes narrowed, probably burning from the smoke.

I gave him a sideways grin.

"We have a problem, you and me."

Curious. "We do? What's that?"

He tugged at a folded sheet of paper tucked into his shirt pocket and passed it to me.

I opened it and immediately recognized the two guys I'd met in Asheville. Had I led them here, and put Lisa in danger?

I raised my eyes to meet Farrow's astute gaze.

"Judging by the look on your face, I'd say you remember these two. They've been sighted in Lexington. I don't know whether they're after you, or Miss Oliver. Or maybe they're just passing through."

A slow breath eased the anxious thoughts assaulting my mind. "So, you don't have eyes on them right now?"

He shook his head. "We haven't actually seen them yet. There's only the anonymous report and then an official sighting. They stopped for gas over on Nicholasville

Road, and one of the local cops recognized them."

Not far away at all. "I see. So why are you here, chatting with me?"

"You have a personal interest in Miss Oliver, I believe."

A personal interest. They had been watching me. I acknowledged his statement with a nod. No use trying to deny it.

"No doubt, she's the reason you were in Richmond but how did you know about Bybee?" He blew out a cloud of smoke.

"Bybee?" I popped another bite of licorice. "Small town I passed through to get to Richmond. I was camping over that way—on the Kentucky River—on assignment."

"Right. Assignment. So, you weren't doing what I asked you not to, following leads on the Olivers when you checked out their former residence?"

"What can I say? I'm a reporter with a natural curiosity, Farrow." I hunched my shoulders. "I was in the neighborhood."

He stood, tossed his cigarette butt on the pavement, and ground it in with the toe of a brown leather wingtip. "More like a dog with a bone. You just can't let it go. So, I'm here to warn you, keep an eye out for these guys."

"I don't guess you'd care to tell me who they are?"

Farrow opened his car door. "Let's just say they're suspects in a major investigation."

I cocked my head. "Armed and dangerous?" I was half-kidding, hoping for a negative response.

He didn't answer, just got in his car and shut the door. "Watch yourself, Bradley. I know you're ex-military, but if you see them, don't engage them." He handed me a card. "Give me a call. Make it official. You can help, or you can hinder."

I played the words over in my mind as I watched the man leave—*Make it official. You can help, or you can hinder*—was he saying what I thought he was saying?

Was he asking for my help?

I pulled into the parking lot of the Bluebird Café. Lisa hadn't arrived, so I cased the lot, checking the plates on the other vehicles. They were all local.

Farrow's visit had me on high alert.

Five minutes passed, and still no Lisa. Would she be there?

I hated that she didn't have a phone. How do people

communicate without a phone? I got out and strode toward the door. I was two steps away when I saw her car approaching.

I waited as she parked and got out and then caught my breath. She looked great. No, better than great, wearing a hot little dress that set fire to her warm, brown eyes. What was that color? Red? Orange?

She tiptoed across the gravel, smiling all the while. "Sorry I'm late, I lost track of time."

"No problem, it was definitely worth the wait." I wiped the silly grin off my face and reached for the door. "Shall we go in?"

She swept past me like an autumn sunset, leaving the scent of honeysuckle behind. Did she have any idea how alluring she was, dressed like that?

We found a table and sat. After ordering our drinks, I watched her. Though she looked great on the outside, something seemed off. I tried but could not read her expression.

She requested another cheeseburger with a cute little smile. "I'm a creature of habit."

"Nothing wrong with that." I ordered the meatloaf, gravy, and mashed potatoes. Comfort food. "So, what do you have, three more weeks until you head back to school?"

She nodded. "Yes, thankfully. I'm so ready to get back." She blew out a sigh.

My gut told me the problem lay with work. "How's work? Did Mr. Sanders bother you this week?"

She glanced out a nearby window. "No."

Avoiding eye contact. What was she trying to hide? Dozens of questions bombarded my journalistic mind, but I suppressed the need to know. For now. When she was relaxed and comfortable, perhaps she would be more forthcoming.

A couple bites of her hamburger warmed her up. She set it down and dabbed at her lips with her napkin. "Where did you end up going this week?"

"Mammoth Cave. And Barren County. Beautiful countryside."

"I've been to Mammoth Cave, a long time ago, with my parents."

I hesitated. This was the first time she had mentioned her parents, except to say they moved a lot. "Were you an only child?"

She drew back. "Is it obvious?"

"Just a guess. You don't really fit the only-child mold, though."

A smile crinkled her nose. "I was a teenager before I realized how different my upbringing was, and I suppose that difference is the reason I don't fit the cliche."

I forked in a bite of mashed potatoes, giving my thoughts time to formulate. "What was different about your upbringing?"

She sat back in her chair. "Everything. Our nomadic existence, Dad's basic distrust of everyone. No one who knew us would describe our family as normal."

Wait. What? *Dad's basic distrust of everyone* . . . why was that? Dare I probe further? I pushed my empty plate away. "So, how did that make you feel, growing up?"

Her lips curved into a gentle smile. "Like an outcast at times. I had to work really hard to make friends in every new situation. And then we'd leave, and I'd have to start all over again."

My eyes were drawn to the door as two patrons entered. An old man in overalls, followed by a younger guy in jeans and cowboy hat. Father and son, no doubt. I tried to relax. If Lisa noticed my nervous reaction to every new customer, she'd think something was up.

The waitress cleared our empty dishes. "Did you save room for dessert? We have blackberry cobbler or pecan pie."

Her hand at her waist, Lisa shook her head. "I have no room."

"Just the check then," I told the waitress. I hated for the meal to end now that Lisa was finally talking about her life. I had tried in vain to figure out a way to get her to say her parents had died without having to ask for the information.

But if I played innocent and she later found out who I was and what I'd been about, she'd never trust me again.

STILL WATER

CHAPTER TWENTY-SEVEN

Lisa

Within seconds of my arrival at the Bluebird, I was convinced, the dress had been a good idea. And the look in Jake's eyes made the price easier to stomach.

Jake had a way of putting people at ease. I supposed that came in handy when he was working. When dinner had ended, and we stepped outside, I found myself hoping he would suggest something. I wasn't sure what, so I hesitated outside the door.

He smiled down at me as he tucked his hair behind his ear. "It's a beautiful evening. Would you like to go for a walk?"

My heart fluttered. I looked around. We were on a main road. A busy one.

He pointed toward the back of the café. "That street is residential. There's a small park at the end. It's a nice, quiet walk."

I faced the direction he had indicated. "All right."

We fell into step together, strolling across the gravel lot until we reached a sidewalk. Would he take my hand? Should I let him?

He didn't. Not yet. Silent for once, hands in his pockets, he kept looking down at me.

Did he suspect I'd had a traumatic day? I had pushed myself hard to cover my hurt and disappointment but somehow it kept rising to the surface. I wanted to tell him everything. His profession kept me silent. An astute journalist could make real trouble for the engineering firm. I didn't want to do that.

I had to *stay below the radar*, as Dad always liked to say. I slanted my gaze toward Jake. We'd been talking about Dad before leaving the café, so I picked it back up. "My dad felt compelled to teach me self-defense."

Jake drew back, half-smiling. "Really? Like Karate or something?"

I nodded. "Or something. I'm not sure, maybe a mix of things. 'You need to know how to protect yourself,' he'd say."

Jake had stopped walking.

I looked up at him.

"So, he really didn't trust people."

I nodded. "Right."

He started forward again and then paused to offer his arm to me. "Is it my imagination, or are you using past tense on purpose when you speak of your father?"

Something about his expression drew me in. We linked arms and started forward. Could I trust him? "He's gone."

"Gone?"

I stared straight ahead but the houses and landscape blurred at the horizon. "He and Mom, they died in a car accident earlier this year."

Jake was silent so long, I dared to glance up at him. His eyes met mine, but I couldn't read his expression. It almost seemed like . . . guilt?

Finally, he spoke. "Lisa, I'm sorry. I . . ." He stopped walking and took a backward step, thrusting his hands into his pockets as though he didn't know what else to do with them.

I filled the silence. "Sometimes, it still seems unreal."

"It would. It will for a long time." He spoke as though he knew the experience. Had he also lost a parent?

We were walking again. Separately. He didn't ask questions, which surprised me a little. I had expected a barrage, and I'd decided to answer. Now I faltered. I didn't know how to begin. Before I could come up with something, he spoke.

"Were they all you have?"

I drew a breath and blew it out. "They were both orphans. Now, I am too."

Jake

The sadness in her eyes shook me to the core. She was finally talking about her parents. I should have been asking questions, getting answers long looked-for, but I had no words. Her sorrow was still too raw. Too deep. It hushed me.

We sat on a stone bench in the small park at the end of the street. Though it was nearly eight-thirty, children still played there. Grownups stood around, visiting with their neighbors.

"You're not completely alone, you know."

Her eyes on mine, she nodded. "And I have school to finish."

"You said your dad never trusted anyone. How has that impacted your life?"

She sighed and fiddled with her purse. "It's hard for me to trust anyone."

Keep it light, Jake. I grinned and leaned closer. "Even me?"

She giggled. "Especially you. Dad instilled in me a basic distrust of men."

That jab hit me square in the gut. I sat back. "Good for him."

She tilted her head. "I always wondered why. I think something must have happened to him, early in life. Something that made him that way. I know so little about his childhood."

I leaned forward and propped my elbows on my knees. "That generation tended to be closed-mouthed about things."

"True. Mom was a classic introvert. She preferred a good book to human interaction."

"That must have been hard for you."

She drew a shaky breath. I was hitting too close to the heart now. Thankfully, a runaway softball bounced a few feet in front of us. I caught it and sent it back in one smooth motion.

I turned back in time to see admiration in her eyes. I grinned. "Yeah, I've still got it."

She laughed. "Did you play baseball?"

"In high school." I stood in front of her and held out my hand. "It'll be dark soon. We'd better start back."

She took my hand and allowed me to help her rise.

We had walked half a block when I realized I still held her hand. It felt natural, so I didn't pull away.

She looked up at me. "What's next for you?"

"Next?"

Her eyes sparkled in the lowering sunlight. "You've seen Mammoth Cave, what can top that?"

"Oh. Well, I don't know. There's that really big lake over in the west, and then there's a natural bridge in the east and Cumberland Falls in the south. I have plenty of choices still available."

"It's good to have choices."

I could see the café sign ahead. My steps slowed. I didn't want our time together to end. Not just for the information I still needed. I was falling fast, and ignoring the alarms going off in my mind became more difficult with each passing moment.

What's your plan, man—a favorite question of my cousin's, who was actually more like a brother—came to mind. For once, I had no plan. I was on the road with no map.

The parking lot was nearly empty. Her car was next to mine. I leaned against my passenger door. "I know it wasn't much, not fancy or anything, but I hope you enjoyed your evening."

She gave me a timid smile. "I did. To be honest, I'm much more comfortable in plain, unassuming surroundings."

I liked that about her. "I wish it wasn't over."

She set her shoulder bag on the hood of the V.W. "I feel like I talked too much about me and my sad, boring life. What about you, Jake? Do you have siblings?"

I tucked my hair behind my ear. "An older sister. She was twelve when I was born, so we weren't really that close. My dad left us when I was ten. Mom went to work at a children's clothing factory. She worked long hours, and attended nursing classes in the evenings, so I usually stayed with my aunt and uncle. My cousins were more like my brother and sister."

She nodded. "I'm sorry you lost your dad so young."

I huffed. "I barely remember him. To tell you the truth, I was probably better off without him. My uncle was Mom's brother. He was a far better man. Kind, and loving.

He and my aunt always made me feel like part of the family. He's the one who got me thinking about the Navy. They were worried I would end up in 'Nam and be killed."

"I love those kinds of stories. I hope to make a difference in someone's life someday."

"Is that why you wanted to teach?"

"Part of the reason."

I sensed something darker behind those words, but now was not the time to pursue it. When she was ready, she'd tell me.

She picked up her purse and found her keys. "I'd better go, it's getting late."

I pushed away from the car and opened her door. "Can we do this again? Or would you like to go somewhere else? I could pick you up next week."

There was that shy smile again. "I'd like that."

Had she really said yes? She was so close I could smell the fresh scent of her hair. More than anything, I wanted to kiss her. My gut told me it was too soon. This was one girl whose trust I needed to gain before I rushed into anything.

So, I took her hand instead. "Do you still have my number in case anything comes up?"

She nodded. "I'll see you Friday."

My heart thrummed louder than my Camaro. Man, I was getting in deep. Maybe too deep.

As I drove toward my place, I remembered Agent Farrow. Had he been somewhere nearby tonight, watching? My growing relationship with Lisa could be the very reason he wanted my help. Maybe when she was with me, he didn't need to worry so much about her safety.

I chuckled, remembering what she said about her dad teaching her self-defense. Maybe she could take care of herself. That was probably something Agent Farrow didn't know.

STILL WATER

CHAPTER TWENTY-EIGHT

Lisa

I pressed the clutch and downshifted. Was I falling in love, or was it only a crush? How could I tell the difference?

I bit my lip to keep from grinning like an idiot. He liked me, too. The way he looked at me and treated me spoke volumes.

Could be wishful thinking on my part, or was I romanticizing? Jake's behavior had not come across as false or in any way seductive, only caring and attentive.

I pulled into the driveway and turned off the engine. I'd never really been in love, so I had nothing to gauge this by.

I got out of the car and walked toward the stairs. The

thought of talking to anyone about my feelings for Jake turned me inside out. I'd never been good at transparency. I would just have to muddle through and hope I didn't make a huge mistake.

Halfway up the steps, Jax jumped out and scared me half to death. I picked her up. She was trembling.

"Oh my gosh, girl. What has gotten into you?" When I set her down on the landing and reached for my key, Jax growled. My skin prickled. I scanned the area. All was quiet, except for moths darting around the dirty bulb overhead. Turning back to the door, another chill shot through me. It was ajar, not closed, and locked, as I had left it.

Straining my ears, I took a backward step. Was someone still inside?

With Ray and Elaine gone, I couldn't even call the police.

I clamped my trembling jaw shut. Someone had broken into my apartment. I pushed the door open with my foot, reached inside, and flipped the light switch. With the kitchen illuminated, I looked around.

Table and chairs overturned, my little radio in pieces on the floor, and some kind of cottony fluff everywhere. What was that?

The closet door stood open. My clothes lay in a heap on the floor. I sucked in a breath. The box! Had they found the attic door and taken the box?

I tossed my purse on the counter. After checking the bathroom to make sure no one was hiding in there, I closed the front door and locked it. As an afterthought, I wedged one of the chairs beneath the knob.

Jax batted at a piece of fluff. My heart throbbed painfully when I realized what it was. My sleeping bag.

Whoever had done this had torn it to bits.

I fought the temptation to fall on my knees and cry. With shaking hands, I forced myself to right the other chair and carry it to the closet. I found my flashlight, climbed up, and pushed the attic door aside. The box was still there. I lowered the door and climbed down.

In one motion, I crumpled and sat with my back against the wall, drew my knees to my chest and wept.

After the sobs subsided, I went in the bathroom and blew my nose, splashed cold water on my face and patted it dry.

Jax drew herself up and sat looking at me with wide eyes.

How I wished she could talk. Judging by her actions outside, she must have seen who had broken in. I looked at the heap of cloth that had been my sleeping bag.

Animals!

Could it have been those two guys Agent Farrow had warned me about? Or was it just neighborhood hoodlums?

No, Ray had said this was a quiet neighborhood, and I'd seen enough of it to know it was.

At least it had been, until I moved in. I had brought this on.

My hands trembled as I fumbled through my purse, seeking Agent Farrow's card. I found it, but I'd have to go to a neighbor's house, or drive up the street to use a pay phone. I didn't want to go anywhere. I wanted to stay right here, curled up like Jax.

My eyes lit on envelopes, ripped apart and scattered. Today's mail. I'd been too distracted to look at it earlier. I gathered it up and took it to the kitchen counter. Under the light, I sifted through the envelopes. It was mostly junk mail, as usual. Then I recognized Mr. Tobey's willowy script. The letter had been torn in half, so I put the pieces together and smoothed them.

"It's wonderful to hear from you, dear. Thea and I are happy to know you are making friends and have found a good job."

I skimmed his usual kind introduction.

"I was able to find the latest travel article you asked for. I'll enclose it with this letter."

I sifted through the pile, looking for a newspaper clipping. I found it, all in one piece. It was titled, "River Camp," with the byline, "Jake Bradley."

I couldn't read it now. I set it aside and picked up the torn letter to see what else Mr. Tobey had to say.

"I was a little dismayed to hear of your acquaintance with the reporter. He seems a nice enough fellow in his writings, but my friend Jim Lewitt told me a reporter named Jake Bradley stopped in at the funeral home not long after you left. The young man wanted information about your parents. Said he was doing a follow-up article on the accident. Of course, Jim didn't tell him anything, but sent him on his way."

Pain stabbed my heart. I shook my head. No, it couldn't be. My vision blurred with unshed tears.

"Do you think he might be the same guy? I'm only telling you this, so you'll be careful, Lisa. You are a young woman all alone, and the wrong kind of person may try to take advantage of that. Stay safe, and God bless you."

God bless me.

I wasn't cold, but I was shaking all over. I sat on the

kitchen floor, put my face in my hands, and rocked forward and back.

"It can't be true. No. Not Jake. Why, God?"

I had finally allowed myself to trust someone. But he was the wrong someone.

When Jax meowed, I forced myself to rise. I opened a can of food and dished a few bites onto her plate.

Something inside me had switched off. I would never be able to stay anywhere. I looked around the room. This was no exception.

I would clean up this mess and pack my things. I'd be gone before daylight, just like my parents.

Just like my parents.

Decided and determined, I removed my sandals, changed into a pair of denim shorts and a navy tee shirt. Crossing to the kitchen sink, I found the folded grocery bags I'd saved and began to clean up all the fluff and debris. I swept the floor, cleaned the bathroom and the kitchen. I packed up the few food items left in the cabinet and cleared the refrigerator.

After carefully folding my clothes, I packed my bag.

Where would I go? I had almost a month until I could move back into the dorm. Though Shelby had invited me to stay with her, that was weeks ago. I didn't even know how to contact her.

I retrieved the shoe box of photos, placed it in the suitcase and then paused. I needed Dad's wallet. I checked inside—the money was still there.

With those two fifties and what I had left from this week's pay, I had a hundred and twenty-eight dollars. Could I survive for a month on that?

Before I replaced the lid, my gaze caught on the small bundle of letters tucked inside. After a moment's consideration, I pulled them out and stuffed them into my purse.

It didn't take long to assemble what was left of my things. A missing item was what concerned me most. My journal.

No trouble packing my car this time, I had so little left. I folded the table and the two chairs and wedged them beside the trash can outside the garage. Heavy-hearted, I climbed the steps one last time.

Leaving had never been easy for me, but this was the worst.

I bent to stroke Jax. "Oh, how I wish I could take you

with me." One day, I told myself. I would settle down, and I could finally have a pet of my own. If I still wanted one.

Back inside, I spent a few minutes writing notes. To Ray and Elaine, I wrote, *Please accept my deepest apologies, but it is necessary for me to leave at this time. You can keep the deposit since I'm leaving without notice.*

I wrote a brief letter of resignation to Mrs. Withery. Then I struggled over a note addressed to Starr.

That one brought a lump into my throat. How I hated leaving such a good friend. I would have to visit her later, during school breaks. *You have been a lifeline.* I paused a moment, as tears threatened again. "Breathe, Lisa." *Please keep praying for me.* I folded the note and sealed it in a separate envelope. I tucked all three letters inside the library book I needed to return.

On Ray's back porch, I put out more food for the cat and used the second can as an anchor for my note.

I surveyed the area as I made my way to the car. A war battled within me. I couldn't stay, but where was I to go? I glanced at the shoebox that I'd put into my passenger seat. The letters from Allison Pearl crossed my mind. The fact that they were three years old was a little daunting, but at least her home had always been inviting.

Maybe it would be again.

As I backed around and pulled out of the drive, I whispered the words Mom used to say, "It's just another adventure. We're turning the page and starting a brand, new chapter."

I had hated it then, and I hated it now.

It was still early morning when I found an inexpensive mom-and-pop motel in Columbia, Tennessee. The manager said he would allow me early occupancy if I paid in advance. I'd driven straight through from Lexington, and though it had been less than five hours, I was dog tired. I hadn't slept since Thursday night.

I lay down on the bed and tried not to think, but all my thoughts swirled around me, looking for a place to light. How could I bear this?

First, the death of my parents, then the loss of almost everything I owned, along with my first real love. A sob caught in my throat.

Jake.

I had responded by doing what my parents had always done. What I had sworn I would never do.

I ran.

STILL WATER

I turned my face into the pillow and wept.

CHAPTER TWENTY-NINE

Jake

Time for a haircut. Past time. The nearest barber shop was packed, but I was happy to wait. I always found them to be great places for conversation.

Feeling at least five pounds lighter, I stopped by the office to check for mail and phone messages. I had both. The phone message from Cran was marked, "STAT."

I made a call to his office first, but I wasn't sure he would be working on Saturday. Cran's assistant suggested I try his home number. I left a quick message on his answering machine. "I'll be here for about an hour."

The phone rang ten minutes later. I was the only one around, so I picked it up.

Cran got right to the point. "I'm glad you called. I

found something I thought may interest you. Did you stop in Plum Springs?"

Plum Springs was the reason I'd visited Barren County after seeing Mammoth Cave. "I did but came up empty. They'd lived in a little travel trailer that has since been moved to make way for a new house. The new owners didn't know anything."

"Well, the next location is a tiny border town called Dukedom."

I grabbed my pen and jotted down the name. "I've heard of it. There's a Dukedom, Kentucky and a Dukedom, Tennessee, depending on where you stand."

"Right. They stayed in an upstairs apartment on the Tennessee side. We actually had a phone number on that one. The owner remembers them. After that, it gets interesting. It was four years back, when the daughter would still be living with them. The location rang a bell with me. I believe I've heard you mention Culleoka, Tennessee."

My jaw dropped. "Are you kidding me? My hometown was a former address for the Olivers?"

"Indeed, it is. I thought that would pique your interest."

Culleoka. I shook my head. "Is this one a box

number?"

"No, it's general delivery."

I nodded. "Yeah, they would've picked up their mail at a little P.O. in a general store. This one will be easy."

"Well, don't get too cocky. Sometimes the easy ones can fool you."

"Don't I know? Is that all you have for me?"

"Well, I'm coming up empty on Oliver's military history. It's as if he never existed. You know what that means."

I rubbed the back of my neck. "Yeah. Either he never served, or he's changed his name along the way."

"Well, we can still narrow it down to a general period of time, but it will take longer."

Leaning back in the chair, I stared at the ceiling. "It'll take luck, too. Like finding the needle in the haystack."

"Have you made any headway with the daughter?"

The memory of her shy smile stirred up an odd mixture of joy and guilt. Not something I should be thinking about right now. I sat forward and tapped my pen on the desk. "Actually yes, but not much I can really use. Mostly what I already knew. They were nomads, and he didn't trust anyone. However, she did confirm they were both orphans. If that's true . . ."

"They would be in the system. But we're not sure of the names, so we're back to the era. It's more of a challenge, but we'll keep looking. You keep doing what you're doing."

I wanted to tell him I'd been caught by the FBI, but that would cost minutes on the line, so I held off. I'd have to find out what Farrow wants first. If he asked for my source, I'd need to keep Cran out of it. In that case, the less said the better.

Once I ended the call with Cran, I had a trip home to plan, hopefully under Farrow's radar, if that was possible. The timing couldn't be more perfect. My cousin in Culleoka had been begging me to visit.

When the phone rang a second time, it was Hamilton's secretary. My trip home would have to wait. I'd been called back to Asheville. Hamilton wanted a new publicity photo and had set up some marketing ops.

I would leave early in the morning, and hopefully be back in town midweek. I wasn't going to let anything interfere with my date Friday night.

Lisa

I was drifting. The sound of water lapping, lapping, lulled me into a deeper, darker place. Something floated on the sparkling water. I wanted to see what it was.

A dead face stared up at me, and I screamed.

I awoke, damp with sweat, and swept my hair from my eyes. The dream, more vivid than ever, tore at my insides. Could it be real? A suppressed memory? Had something happened to me when I was a young child?

At a tender age, finding a drowning victim would have been devastating. A trauma like that, if it had really happened, would solve a lot of my unanswered questions and perhaps explain my parents' behavior, too.

I missed my journal, where I could write my feelings and keep them close. I'd wracked my brain, trying to remember what I'd written last. Had there been anything that someone could use against me? But why would they want to? Who were these people?

A long, slow breath settled my nerves.

Somewhat rested after my three-hour nap, I got up and took a shower. I made a peanut butter and honey sandwich and sat in a chair to eat it. The first bite was hard to swallow. I missed Jax's begging at my feet. I popped open a can of soda and sipped.

Forcing my thoughts away from the nightmare, I concentrated on the present circumstances. I was nearly home. The last home that I'd known before college anyway. It seemed strange to think of this as home, since I'd only lived here a year and that was over three years ago. But there was something about this place. I had been happy here.

I sat back in my chair and contemplated the days ahead. I would find my friends and see if they could put me up for a few days. That is, if they were still my friends after I'd never answered Allison's letters. It was probably presumptive of me, maybe even rude, but I was desperate. Besides, Elsie Pearl had always been known to take in strays. Many of the neighborhood kids had called her "Mama Pearl."

Right now, I was banking on her goodness and grace. I would even go to church with her if she asked.

By a quarter past three, I had tired of being trapped in that small room with only my tragic thoughts for company. I contemplated calling the Pearls, even planned the conversation, repeating it over and over in my mind.

I lifted the receiver but couldn't dial the number. Instead, I grabbed my keys and headed for the car.

Columbia on a Saturday was a busy place. I stuck to side streets, just sightseeing. I noticed only a few changes. A new shop in the main square drew my attention. I parked and went inside. Maybe I could find a new journal. Even a notebook would suffice. They had both. The notebook was cheaper, so I bought it. When I left the store, I noticed a little café a few doors down.

I wasn't ready to visit another diner. Too many memories of Jake, but I was hungry, so I stopped and ordered a burger and fries to go.

It was nothing like the Bluebird. The decor reminded me of a fifty's diner. It was cool, and sleek with a lot of chrome. Though bustling, the staff was small-town friendly.

I sat at the counter and sipped soda while waiting for my order. Most of the tables were full and several waitresses rushed back and forth. I was still quite tired, but my senses were on high alert, so I was very much aware when someone stopped and stood next to me.

"Lisa Oliver? Is that really you?"

I swiveled on the stool to face a slightly older version of Bucky Thompson, one of my high school classmates.

Same strawberry blond hair and freckles, same quirky humor in his eyes.

I smiled. "Bucky?"

He gave a low chuckle. "Nobody calls me that anymore. He held out his hand. "It's Will."

I shook his work-roughened hand and kept the contact brief and businesslike. "Will, it's great to see you. Are you still living in the area?"

He nodded. "Working at the new auto plant in Springfield. There's several of us over there."

"Are you still playing ball?"

His eyes flashed when he grinned. "Good memory. A local team, just for fun."

So, he hadn't achieved his dream of playing pro-ball, though from the looks of it, he'd stayed in shape.

He leaned an elbow on the counter. "What're you doing in town, or should I ask?"

I made eye contact. What had he meant by that? "I was passing through and thought I'd visit."

Holding my gaze, he nodded. "We've wondered about you every once in a while."

I tilted my head. "We?"

He nodded. "You remember Allison? We're getting married in the spring."

I faked a wide-eyed innocent look of surprise, though my true emotion came closer to shock. "Really? Congratulations."

Allison and Bucky. Never would I have put those two together.

"Yes, I remember she was kind of miffed when you never wrote her back."

One of the waitresses set a to-go bag on the counter. "Here's your food, Miss. Thanks for stopping by."

I nodded as Will's words sank in. "I didn't receive the letters."

He gave me a sideways glance as though he didn't believe me.

I picked up the bag and slid off the stool. "I wondered why she hadn't written, when she seemed so excited about the prospect of keeping in touch." No sense telling Will that Mom hadn't given me the letters. That was a conversation I needed to have with Allison first, to explain and ask forgiveness.

He gestured toward the door. "I'm on my way out, too. I'll walk you to your car."

I led him toward the V.W.

"No way! You're still driving that thang?" He slid a palm over the hood. "Looks like you've kept her in good shape."

I opened the driver's side door and grinned. "It's a classic."

He nodded. "It sure is. Hey—how long will you be around? Maybe we can get together. With Allison, of course."

Good thing he had added that last part, though I wondered if Allison would want to see me. Now that I'd talked to Will, doubts crowded in. I cleared my throat. "I had planned to visit them tomorrow after church."

"Where are you staying, that new motel on Springfield Road?"

I shook my head. "The old one by the college."

Will nodded and gave me a thumb's-up. "Ah. Classic. I got you." He thumped the hood with his knuckles. "Well, I'll let her know you're back in town."

"Thanks, Will." I got in, and he shut the door.

He lifted his hand in farewell. "If we don't see you again, take care, OK?"

I couldn't say thanks again, it would sound too dorky, so I nodded instead. Looks like I'd be having a cold hamburger and fries for supper tonight.

CHAPTER THIRTY

Lisa

Trucks passed in the night. A whistle blew, followed by one of the longest trains I had ever heard. I missed the quiet neighborhood. I missed Jax. I turned over and faced the wall, trying not to think about who else I missed, and prayed for sleep.

Sunlight filtered through the fiberglass curtains when I awoke. I squinted at the clock. Eight-thirty, nine-thirty back home.

I sat up and yawned. A full night's sleep with no nightmares. After a hot shower, I put on my white shorts and pink top. Then I remembered it was Sunday. The Pearls were old-fashioned, so I traded the shorts for a navy skirt. I was putting my makeup on when the phone rang. I froze. Who would call me here?

I sat on the edge of the bed and lifted the receiver. "Hello?"

"Is this Lisa?"

My ears perked up at the familiar voice. "Yes."

"Hi, it's Allison."

"I thought that was you. How are you?" Keep it polite, not too warm.

"I was so surprised when Will told me he'd seen you. I hope you have time for a visit. Mom would love to see you, too."

Her voice seemed friendly. Could be southern hospitality, though. I had fallen for that in the past. "Umm, yes, I suppose I could stop by." And maybe stay a couple of weeks? Was that asking too much?

"Oh yes, please do. I have a million questions."

Frankly, so did I. Not that I had any answers.

A familiar voice in the background announced, "Tell Lisa to come for Sunday dinner. One o'clock. I'm making her favorite."

Allison chuckled. "You heard?"

I smiled at the thought of Elsie Pearl's chicken and dumplings. "I did. Tell your mother I'll be there."

"Okay. We're headed out to church in a bit. Mom said

to come with us if you can. I'm sure you remember where it is."

Church. "I . . ." searched in vain for an excuse, leaving only dead air between us. I had sort of made a promise to myself that I would go if Elsie asked. Funny how quickly my resolve dissolved.

Allison laughed. "Don't worry about it, Lisa. I told Mom I would ask, is all. We'll talk later, okay? I can't wait to see you."

After she hung up, I sat for a moment, replaying the conversation in my mind. Maybe all was forgiven?

She had said there was a lot to talk about and boy, was she right. Besides all the water under my bridge, Allison was engaged. To Bucky—uh—Will. They seemed an odd couple, but maybe he had changed. He certainly seemed more mature, even respectful.

I got up and crossed to the bathroom to finish getting ready. One o'clock would give me time to check out of the motel and grab a coffee at that café. Assuming they were open on Sunday.

I picked up my suitcase and carried it to the car and then headed to the office to turn in my key.

"I hope you enjoyed your stay," the manager said with a friendly smile as I headed for the door.

"I did, thank you." One thing about the south, everyone was friendly and usually courteous. I had missed that.

I cut through a side street lined by grand old houses. Turning on Main, I was relieved to find the open sign in the window of the café.

A coffee to-go in hand, I returned to my car. Blue skies overhead tempted me to take a stroll. Churches were still in session. Only the occasional car passed by on the street. But what if someone should recognize me? I certainly hadn't expected to bump into Will Thompson.

Being sighted by the locals wasn't my greatest concern. Even though I was certain I hadn't been followed, I couldn't be a hundred percent sure I was home free. If my troubles followed me here, and my friends were in any way endangered, I would never forgive myself.

Lisa

The Pearls lived in an unincorporated, rural community, about fifteen minutes south of Columbia. Their fifties' era, red brick ranch-style house was located on Sun Drop Lane. I pulled into the drive and sat for a moment, taking it all in. I had always liked this house. It was more modern than most of the places my family chose.

Every weekday morning, I'd run across the one-lane road to join Rick and Allison for the short drive to school. The brother and sister had treated me like family. I suppose that's the reason I had bonded with them so quickly.

The front door opened, and Allison stepped onto the small concrete porch, her hand lifted in a tentative wave.

I got out and grabbed my purse. Nerves fluttered in my tummy as she walked toward me. She wore the same hairstyle, long, blond hair, straight and silky, tucked behind her right ear.

Looping my purse strap over my shoulder, I met her halfway. "Hello, Allison."

Her blue eyes seemed darker. Perhaps it was the uncertainty that shone so plainly on her face. "You haven't changed a bit. Come on in."

Petite but wiry, Elsie Pearl reminded me of a mother hen, stretching her wings over every stray that stepped through her door. Like me at that moment.

"It is so wonderful to see you." She almost sang the words as she wrapped her arms around me and kissed my cheek. "We've missed you so much."

Closing my eyes, I allowed myself to bask in the woman's affection. My parents had never been demonstrative. I had never doubted their love, but sometimes I longed for a hug like this one. Now, I didn't want it to end.

When Elsie released me, I took in her appearance. Her light brown hair held a bit more gray, but her hazel eyes still sparkled with energy.

"Y'all come hang out with me while I finish dinner." She flitted past me toward the kitchen.

With a knowing smile, Allison took my purse and hung it on a hook inside the coat closet. I'd always liked their habit of hanging their purses on those hooks. It kept them handy. You never had to wonder where they were.

I drank in the familiar decor of the home as I trailed behind Elsie. The same antique Tiffany lamp on a table in the living room window, the formal dining room already set for dinner, and finally, the center of their home, a big, country kitchen. Warm. Homey. Comfortable.

Elsie picked up a spoon and stirred a pot of simmering goodness. "Lisa, have a seat at the breakfast bar. Allison, fix Lisa a glass of iced tea, please."

I bit my lip to keep from smiling. Elsie was always

issuing orders. No one minded since they were given with kindness.

Ice cubes clinked and then crackled as the liquid poured over it. Allison handed me a glass. I smiled in anticipation of the cold, syrupy liquid I'd learned to love, especially on a hot, summer afternoon.

Elsie hummed as she moved around the kitchen, intent on her cooking.

I set my glass down. "Everything looks just the same."

"Why change perfection?" Elsie held a spoon toward Allison. "Does this need more salt, love?"

Allison tasted the broth. "Maybe a dash. It's nearly perfect." She picked up her tea and sat next to me. "I'm so glad you came."

"Did you think I wouldn't?"

She ran a finger around the lip of her glass. "Will said you didn't receive my letters."

I took another sip, wondering how to begin. What I had to say would upset them, but there was no alternative. "I didn't, until recently."

"Recently? I sent them to the address your mother gave me. It's been three years."

I watched her expression. "Did you lose the address I gave you?"

She shook her head. "Your mother said there'd been a change. She gave me the new one and said to send any letters there."

Elsie faced us. "You probably still have that card Mrs. Oliver gave you." She looked at me. "She came over here the day after you left, and said you'd called and given her the new information."

Mom hadn't just failed to give me the letters, she had outright lied. I took a deep breath and slowly blew it out.

Allison touched my arm. "You said you got them, though, recently?"

I gave a slow nod. "I have no idea why Mom did that. I suppose she had her reasons."

For a moment, we were all silent. I was uncertain how to tell them. Should I just blurt it out?

Elsie tilted her head to the side. A frown creased her brow. "How is your mother, Lisa?"

I took a deep breath and forced myself to meet her gaze. "Mom and Dad were killed in a car accident this past April."

One of them gasped, I was not sure which. Mother hen spread her wings and enveloped me in her fix-everything hug.

Allison rubbed my back. "I'm so sorry. What a terrible

thing to go through."

Still holding me, Elsie kissed my brow. "And you, all alone. Honey, that just breaks my heart."

In retrospect, I probably should have held my announcement until after dinner.

The back door opened, and feet stomped on the porch. Before he entered the kitchen, I knew it was Riley Pearl, whom everyone called Pop, coming in from the barn.

Allison's dad looked from one to the other of us, before he nodded at me. "Lisa, good to see you." Rather than add to whatever was happening, he stepped to the sink and washed his hands. Smart man.

I wanted to laugh out loud. What must he be thinking?

Elsie released me but kept her hand on my shoulder. "Dinner's ready. Y'all all grab something and head on in."

I picked up my glass and a basket of dinner rolls.

Armed with potholders, Pop took the still bubbling pot of chicken and dumplings and set it on a trivet in the middle of the dining room table.

Once we were all seated, he prayed over the meal, finishing with a blessing for me. "And Lord, bless Miss Lisa. Thank you for bringing her safely home."

Home. There was that word again.

Each of us in turn held our bowl for Elsie to fill.

Allison passed the bread to me. I took a roll and passed the basket to Pop.

"Lisa, are you still in college?" He asked, between bites.

"Yes, I have one more year."

He nodded. "I'm glad you were able to stay with it."

Though he had missed that part of the conversation, I'd seen Elsie whisper something in his ear. So, I didn't hesitate to talk about it.

"The accident happened shortly after I'd returned from spring break. I didn't have much time to think about it before finals."

Allison shook her head. "That must have been so hard for you."

Guilt coursed through my veins as I looked at all their faces. "I'm sorry to spring all this on you at mealtime."

"Oh, don't you worry about that," Pop said. "We're all family here. Mama, pass me the rolls, please."

Elsie passed the basket to her husband before turning to me. "Where have you been living since school let out?"

"I was in Lexington. But now, I ... well, I guess you'd say I'm between addresses. Until school starts, anyway."

Allison frowned. "You mean you don't have anywhere to live? You have almost a month before school starts."

"I'm taking some time off before I go back." What would they think if they knew the truth, that Mom and Dad's death had been ruled a double homicide, and now the suspects may be after me? Yikes. Probably best if I didn't tell them that part.

Elsie got up to refill Pop's glass. "Well, your timing couldn't be more perfect. I hope you'll stay with us for a few days, or at least through next weekend. We're having an engagement party for Allison and Will."

"Oh, yes," Allison said. "Please stay. I'd love it more than anything. And Rick's coming home. I know he'd love to see you."

I happily accepted their kind invitation. Procuring it had been easier than expected. The cocktail of emotions swirling around inside my heart however, I had not anticipated.

STILL WATER

CHAPTER THIRTY-ONE

Lisa

After dinner, Allison and I walked arm-in-arm behind Elsie and Pop, who wanted to show me his new "fishin' lake."

It was more like a large pond, but I humored Pop by showing proper amazement. He'd built a sturdy dock and added some landscaping that included a two-person swing beneath a big, old maple tree.

Pop and Elsie stopped there.

Elsie waved us on. "Show Lisa your house, honey."

Allison led me along a well-worn path that hugged the lake shore where we stopped to watch as a couple of ducks glided across the pond.

The dark water reminded me of my dream, so I turned

my back on it and instead filled my vision with rolling, green fields where Pop's cattle grazed. "It's beautiful out here."

Allison twirled a bright green sassafras leaf between her fingers. "I know. It's so peaceful."

"Are you working anywhere?"

She shook her head. "Will doesn't want me to work. Right now, he's making a good salary."

I could easily imagine her staying home, raising a family, just like her mother.

The bare frame of a new house stood on a rise above the lake. Allison's eyes shone as she pointed out the rooms. Then, in the middle of what would one day be her living room, she spun around with outstretched arms. Pure joy.

I didn't really envy her, but I did experience something I'd never felt before. It was almost like an inexpressible wish for something I never expected to have. A home, a family . . . love.

I forced a polite response. "I'm sure it's going to be lovely."

She touched my arm. "You'll have to come and visit. We'll have a guest room all ready for you."

I tried to ignore the painful jab in my heart. Though I

liked the idea of visiting her in the future, an ugly, dark cloud still hung over me.

"Just like old times," Allison whispered from her bed across from mine. "Remember that night after the homecoming dance? We giggled so loud, Pop said he was going to send us to the barn."

I smiled at the memory of that and all the other nights I had spent in this room with its dusty rose walls and fluffy ivory comforters on the twin beds. I had been so envious of such luxury. "I do remember. He would've done it, too."

She was silent so long, I thought she had fallen asleep. When she spoke, her voice wavered. "I'm so sorry."

"For what?"

"If I had mailed the letters to the address you gave me, we might have still been close, and then you wouldn't have been alone when you lost your parents."

I breathed out a sigh. "That's a lot of ifs and would haves. I don't blame you. How could you possibly know? I'm sorry you had to go through that. Waiting for my letters. Wondering why I didn't write back. That must have been hard for you."

"It was. But as soon as I saw your face this morning, I knew everything would be okay. I'm so glad you're home. I hope you'll come back for the holidays. Thanksgiving, Christmas, and New Year's. Remember staying up all night on New Year's Eve?"

I laughed. "I sure do. I don't know about Thanksgiving, though. I guess it depends on how well I keep up with my classes. But I'd love to come for winter break, if you think it will be all right."

"You know how Mama loves to entertain. She'll be so excited. Have you thought about what you'll do after graduation? Are you still planning to teach?"

"I'm not sure. With all that's happened, I'm undecided."

"That's understandable. It will all work out when the time comes. That's how God is. Sometimes you can't see what lies ahead, and then the door opens and there it is."

I chuckled. "You sound so old and wise."

"Well, I'll be an old married woman before long."

Quiet fell over us again. Soon, her even breathing told me she had fallen asleep, I contemplated her words, *everything would be okay*. Would it ever be okay for me?

For a few weeks in Lexington, I had been almost happy. Once the heaviness of loss began to abate, I'd dared to believe I could have a normal life. I even began to let myself fall in love with Jake. I had trusted him.

What a fool I'd been.

I'd let someone in, even after all Dad's warnings. Had Jake been responsible for the break-in? My heart said no, but doubts remained.

Dark water swirled around me. All my losses floated on the surface, taunting me. Reminding me I could never be free. Worst of all, I was a coward. Like my father before me, I ran away.

I turned my face to the wall, closed my eyes, and waited for sleep.

The murmur of quiet voices in another room greeted my waking moments. I turned over and squinted at the clock. Ten minutes after nine, that was ten at home.

Showered and dressed, I headed for the kitchen. When I passed Rick's room, I stopped and stood in the doorway. It was a blast from the past, almost like he was still there. His favorite football team poster hung on the wall, along with ribbons and awards from his years on the high school football team and the same brown, plaid bedspread topped the bed. He'd thrown one of those pillows at me once. I almost giggled aloud at the memory.

He'd had a crush on me, but I didn't have feelings for him beyond friendship. I thought he was cute, but we just didn't match. That was something the younger me couldn't figure out how to express. He was hurt and even angry for a time. But by graduation, he had forgiven me.

Leaving the past behind, I followed my nose to the kitchen.

Allison was seated at the bar sipping coffee. She looked up when I entered. "Morning, Lisa."

"Good morning. That bacon smells wonderful."

Elsie reached for me. "Good morning, sunshine."

I submitted to an Elsie hug and a peck on the cheek. *I could get used to this.*

"I hope you slept well."

"Yes, ma'am. I didn't mean to sleep so long. I know you're usually up with the chickens."

She patted my cheek. "Don't you worry about it. I want you to take it easy while you're here. And we need to put some meat on those bones, so you won't freeze this winter."

Allison brought me a cup of coffee. "We've been finalizing our plans for Saturday."

I thanked her for the coffee and perched on a stool at the bar. "How many guests are you expecting?"

She passed me the cream decanter. "A couple dozen or so. Mainly family, close friends, and neighbors."

"A couple dozen or so. That's about fifty in southern-speak." I grinned when Elsie giggled.

Allison cracked eggs into a bowl and stirred the contents with a whisk. "You'll recognize some of them from school."

Even with no makeup and her hair pulled back in a messy ponytail, she was beautiful. Allison had been popular at school, something I'd only dreamed of. I was always the weirdo outcast. At least I had been, until Allison took me under her wing.

Elsie forked the last few pieces of bacon onto a plate. "Pops built a barbecue pit down by the lake. There's plenty of shade and lots of room for the kids to play."

Allison handed the bowl of eggs to her mother.

I noticed there were only three place settings on the kitchen table. "Is Pop at work?"

Allison nodded. "He's on the early shift at the dairy, and then comes home and works a full day here."

"Is he still raising beef cattle?"

"Yes, along with a few pigs." Elsie handed a platter of

biscuits to Allison. "You can set these on the table, hon."

I slid off the stool and carried my cup to the table. Pop also grew corn and soybeans and Elsie kept hens for the eggs they produced. The two of them led busy lives. I had to admire their energy. No wonder they had kept their trim figures as they had aged.

"So, who lives across the road now?"

Elsie offered me a biscuit. "A sweet family with three youngsters and two big dogs. You'll probably meet them this week. The children spend most of their waking hours outdoors. The oldest boy sometimes fishes at Pop's lake."

Allison passed a bowl of Elsie's homemade strawberry jam my way. "And Mr. George's cows still end up in both our yards from time to time."

I smiled at the memory. "He never fixed that fence?"

Elsie cackled. "Of course not. It's an ongoing joke." She set her cup down and smiled at me. "I'm so glad you're here, sugar. I hope you'll stay until you have to go back to school. What you need is time to rest and recover from all that's happened to you. Then you'll be ready to hit those books and finish strong."

A lump clogged my throat. "I don't know what to say."

Allison took my hand. "Just say, 'I'd love too, thank you very much.'"

I smiled. "I'd love to. Thank you for such a kind invitation."

"Well, that's the last one you're going to get," Elsie said, with a straight face.

I looked from one to the other, waiting for some sign that Elsie was teasing me.

She chuckled. "I'm kidding, hon. From now on, this is your home. You just come on back any time. No need to ask first, just show up. I'll have Pop get you a key."

STILL WATER

CHAPTER THIRTY-TWO

Jake

Good thing I'd already gotten that haircut. Hamilton's schedule included a photo shoot first thing Monday morning. I endured nearly an hour of hair, makeup, and wardrobe.

Yes, wardrobe.

They put me in a three-piece charcoal suit first and finished up with jeans and a leather jacket. I preferred the latter.

Next, I had a quick face-to-face with Hamilton before heading to a local television station for an interview with Tammy Trinkle, their morning show hostess. She reminded me of a hungry piranha. I think I defended myself well.

"Jake, you were virtually unknown until earlier this year when *Jake on the Road* made its debut. How are you handling sudden fame?"

"It hasn't really sunk in yet. I'm as amazed as anyone at the way the column took off. So, I really don't feel like I've handled anything, other than a change in wardrobe." I fingered the lapel of my new, gray suit and gave Tammy Trinkle a big smile.

I heard a few snickers among the crew, but Tammy ignored my attempt at humor. Instead, she stuck to the prompted lines. "So, was the idea for the column all yours, or was it an assignment—someone else's brainchild?"

"I can't take credit for the idea. My editor, Alan Hamilton, of the *Asheville Summary*, came up with that on his own. I just wrote the articles."

Tammy smiled at the camera. "You just wrote the articles. Well, you definitely have a gift, Mr. Bradley."

"Thank you, Tammy." Since my charm was wasted on Miss Trinkle, I smiled into the camera.

She looked down her nose at me. "I have to confess I had never even heard of your column until last week. I gave it a read and found it entertaining."

Entertaining. I wanted to tell her what I thought of her morning broadcasts. Instead, I nodded as though I understood completely. "I suppose stories about the great outdoors, mom-and-pop restaurants, and roads-less-traveled won't appeal to everyone."

"Judging by the growing readership, I suppose you do have a few fans out there."

More like a few thousands, so I'm told. "Well, believe me, I'm grateful for every one of those." I eyed the camera again.

She nodded and gave me a warm smile. "If you continue to write at the same level, telling heartwarming and even funny stories—like last week's—what was it?"

I was almost convinced that I'd made an impression on her until she said that. "A Horse's Tale."

Tammy chortled. "Your sense of humor does translate well to the written word."

"Thank you, Tammy."

She closed with, "What's next for Jake Bradley?"

"Lunch, I hope." After a chorus of chuckles from the crew, I gave her a serious answer. "Possibly a book, if I can convince anyone to publish it."

"On travel? I would love to read more about your adventures in some of those backwater towns."

Hmm. Well, that wasn't the book I had in mind. I longed to write a completely different story of danger and deception, but I couldn't tell anyone about that one. Not yet.

After the interview, I wolfed down a fast-food burger and hoofed it on back to the office for another meeting with Hamilton.

He jumped right in. "How'd it go?"

"Well, I think. She seemed to like my stories and made the best of them."

"Good. Now, what's happening with the other thing?"

"I'm making slow progress."

"I thought you were going to be my star investigative reporter, Bradley. You need to speed things up. Find out as much as you can. Then we're going to have to back off."

What? I frowned. "Back off?"

He rubbed his forehead. "I've had a visit from that guy, Farrow. He still insists there is no story and even if we do find something, we can't print it. Besides raising my hackles nearly to the boiling point, he elevated my curiosity." He slapped the desk with an open hand. "I want you to find out what they're trying to cover up."

He shot from his chair and paced to the window. He paused, looking out the dirty glass for a few moments before he took it up again. "However, when you're warned by the authorities to back off, you have to at least appear to do so."

He turned to face me. "Which is what I'm telling you right now. But before we let it go, get as much information on record as possible."

I could do that. "Did you tell Agent Farrow I'm not officially on the story?"

"I didn't bother to deny my interest. That guy's got a better nose than a bloodhound. I take it you've heard from him as well?"

"He found me in Lexington, gave me a warning." I didn't tell Hamilton that Farrow had hinted that I could help him. I figured my best plan was to stay aboveboard and play nice.

"Well, that's another reason I brought you in. I thought it might throw him off your scent. Make him think I've officially put the brakes on."

Once again, Farrow's insisting there was no story made me want to dig deeper, especially after what Cran had told me. If the Olivers had reinvented themselves at some point, there was most definitely something to be found.

I left Hamilton's office with Tuesday's schedule in hand. It looked like I wouldn't be home until late Wednesday, which was fine with me. I had several weeks of travel posts already written and turned in.

On the way back to my Asheville apartment, I stopped at a local grocery to pick up some empty boxes. I'd decided to let my apartment go. I could use that money elsewhere.

Besides, there were . . . things . . . in Lexington that I couldn't seem to get out of my mind.

It was always slow-going on Jellico Mountain, just over the Kentucky state line. Semis tended to bunch up on the steep incline, and it was nearly impossible to get around them.

About halfway up, I noticed a black Dodge Challenger closing in. As the incline leveled out, I sped up. So did the other driver.

Suspecting a tail, I took the first available exit. I didn't like to drive too fast on these back roads. They were nearly as dangerous as those near Asheville. Also, cops tended to target me. The downside of driving a muscle car.

At first, I didn't see the other vehicle, so I turned left onto a narrow lane and looked for a place to turn around. I was headed back out with a hundred yards or so between me and the main highway when I saw the Dodge drive by at a high rate of speed. With a little luck, the driver hadn't noticed me on my detour.

A few minutes later, I was back on track with no apparent tail. Not far up the road, I switched over to Highway 25, even though it would add another hour to my trip.

At a quarter past seven, I pulled into the parking lot of my monthly-rate motel room in Lexington. Felt good to be back, though I tamped down my temptation to drive past Lisa's place. With her work hours, she was probably already asleep.

I unloaded most of my boxes before I sat down and called Farrow's number. It was getting late, and I did not want to put this conversation off any longer.

He answered right away. "Agent Farrow."

"Well, hello, Agent Farrow, it's Jake Bradley. I just returned from a trip to Asheville. You probably already knew that. I had to shake a tail near the state line."

Farrow chuckled. "You've overrated your importance, Bradley. I wouldn't waste time and resources on your shenanigans. You went back home. Did you get fired?"

"I hate to disappoint you, but no, my editor wanted me to do some marketing, promoting my popular travel column. So, you're not interested in me at all?"

"Didn't say that. Where's your girlfriend?"

"My girlfriend? You mean Miss Oliver? At her apartment, I assume." I *had* assumed. Was she gone?

Farrow sighed. "She pulled a disappearing act, just like her old man used to do."

My back went ramrod straight. "Lisa disappeared? When?"

"We figure in the wee hours, Saturday morning."

Saturday morning, that was right after . . . our date. "H—How do you know she's gone? Maybe she just took a trip."

"She's gone. Place was cleaned out. And the owners were off on a vacation. She left them a note and some very interesting garbage."

"Garbage? You went through her garbage?"

"No stone unturned. It's like she'd torn her stuff up, or maybe someone else did." His voice rose an octave. "You don't know anything about that, do you?"

I shook my head as if Farrow could see me.

Someone else? "What about those guys you were looking for? Maybe they . . ." I swallowed, hard. Had they abducted Lisa? "What about her car?"

"Gone. No, we suspect she took herself out of there. Maybe she arrived home and found the place trashed. It would've spooked her."

"I don't know. I can't see her skipping out on college. She only has one more year. It's important to her."

"We checked there first. It's still almost three weeks until she can move into the dorm. You two have been all cozy lately, I was hoping you'd heard from her." After a long pause, he added, "I just want to make sure she's safe, Bradley."

"I haven't heard from her. I really didn't know she was gone." And that bothered me. "What about her college roommate? She offered—"

"We checked. No one home. The family's away for a month."

Coming up empty, I rubbed my chin. She had that friend at work. "I can check around."

Anticipating my line of thought, Farrow added, "She also left a note at her workplace."

"I see." Still, her friend may know something.

"Keep me posted, Bradley."

I almost laughed out loud. "Will you keep me posted?"

"Let's see what happens, and we'll go from there."

I hung up.

Lisa had gone.

I paced the narrow path between all the boxes in the room. It was too late to check my P.O. Box, but maybe I had a letter, too.

No. I rubbed the back of my neck. She wouldn't know about my P.O. Box. She didn't even know where I lived. How had I managed to lose her, just when we were getting closer? At least I thought we were developing a bond. She'd seemed receptive to the idea of a real date.

If only I'd followed her home. Had those two goons been in her apartment when she arrived? My pulse sped up at the thought. If they had hurt her—but no—Farrow didn't think so. It looked to him like Lisa cleaned the place out and left in the middle of the night.

It made sense. It was what she knew to do.

I stopped pacing, threw myself on the bed and stared at the ceiling. It was her dad's fault. He'd trained her too well. A normal person would find the nearest phone and report a break-in, file a report. But not Bill Oliver's kid, she'd feel compelled to handle it on her own.

She had my number, why hadn't she called?

What was it Farrow said, they'd torn up the place? Maybe she didn't have the number anymore. Maybe she hadn't known how to get hold of me.

CHAPTER THIRTY-THREE

Jake

I'd just finished shaving when someone knocked at my door. I shrugged into a tee shirt and then peeked through the drapes to see who was there.

A man in a suit—Farrow. I opened the door. Before I could speak, he indicated I should come outside.

"You really need to rethink your transportation, Bradley." He nodded toward my car.

Both doors were ajar. The trunk was open. I sucked in a breath. "Oh, man!"

Farrow shook his head. "I know. I was passing by, saw the car, and thought I'd better let you know."

When I stepped toward my vehicle, he held up his hand. "Don't touch anything. I have a team on the way."

"A team? Really?"

"We need tangible evidence in order to hold those two goons."

"So, you think this is their handiwork? Are they responsible for Lisa's place, too?"

"Not ready to say that." He shoved his hands in his pockets. "I can't talk to you about the case, so don't bother asking questions."

I lowered my voice. "I'm not going to write about it, Farrow. I just want to know."

"I'm sure you do. Still can't tell you anything. But your friend—the one who's doing your footwork for you—should have some valuable info in a day or two."

I arched my brows. Was he acquainted with Cran? I clamped my mouth shut, though, in case it was a ploy to get me talking.

He chuckled. "You are so predictable, Bradley. If you're going to play this game, you need to do your homework. It wouldn't hurt to take a course in subterfuge."

Had he just insulted me?

He pointed a thumb at the Camaro. "You might as well hang a billboard on your car. Not hard to spot. You need something nondescript."

"Are you in your weird, roundabout way actually encouraging me to keep up the chase?"

He cracked a smile. "With a little preening, you could become a topnotch investigative reporter. Or a detective. Probably more money in your brand of journalism, though."

I watched over his shoulder as a black sedan pulled in. Must be his "team."

Two suits got out of the vehicle. The driver grabbed a case from the back seat.

Without a word to me, Agent Farrow turned and walked toward my car.

I kept my distance, but never took my eyes off the men as they combed my vehicle for possible clues. Half an hour passed before Farrow waved me over to the open trunk of my car. "Is anything missing, Mr. Bradley?"

I looked inside and then shook my head. "Nothing."

Farrow crossed his arms over his chest as he leveled a gaze at me. "So, you're saying that whatever you normally carry in the trunk of your car is not missing?"

I peered at him through narrowed eyes. What was he getting at? "What I'm saying is, I cleaned my car out yesterday. What I usually carry is stored in my room."

Farrow relaxed his stance. "In your room. All right."

He gestured to the men. "We're done here." To me, he said, "You can have your car back."

I lowered my head and muttered, "Okay, then."

Farrow's dynamic duo got in their vehicle and drove away.

I closed my trunk. When I turned, I expected to see Farrow leaving, too.

Instead, he leaned against his car.

I thought about grabbing a licorice twist.

He didn't light a cigarette, however, he just stood there looking at me. "Be on your guard, Bradley."

"Against what?"

His smile didn't quite make it to his eyes. "Can't say. Don't leave just yet. Not tonight, anyway. Early tomorrow morning is probably best."

I perked up. He had my attention. I had not told him I was going anywhere, yet he knew. How had he known? *Don't leave yet.* It sounded like an order. "Is that all?"

He pulled a pack of cigarettes from his breast pocket, removed one and placed it between his lips but didn't light it. After replacing the pack, he lit the cigarette and then spoke around it. "And consider ditching that muscle car for the time being."

He got in his black sedan and started the engine.

Without another word, he backed around and pulled out of the parking lot.

Though I'd hoped to head home to Tennessee this afternoon, I delayed according to Farrow's advice.

No messages waited for me at the office, so I drove by Addison-Allegro Engineers, Lisa's former workplace. Upon arrival, however, I changed my mind about looking for her friend. With all their rules, I'd never make it past the front desk. Returning around five made more sense.

The Bluebird was my next stop for a late lunch. Trudy wasn't working, so I couldn't interrogate her about Lisa's whereabouts. I used the time to jot down a few possible questions for Lisa's coworkers, assuming someone would talk to me.

With two hours to kill, I headed to the office to work on a couple of columns. Russell was out. I had the place to myself. I wasted several sheets of paper before giving up. Thoughts of Lisa consumed me. Where was she?

An hour later, I stood outside Addison-Allegro, hoping to catch Lisa's friend, Starr. I'd seen them walk out together the day I'd met Lisa here.

The young woman was among the first to exit. She headed for a tan Pontiac parked on the street.

I called out to her. "Excuse me, are you Starr?"

She paused and looked toward me. However, she didn't respond.

Taking a step nearer, I smiled. "I'm Lisa's friend, Jake. I was wondering if you'd heard from her."

She opened her mouth and then hesitated.

An older lady got out of the tan car. "Starr, you coming?"

Starr still didn't move. She looked at the woman and then back at me.

I held my ground. "I'm worried about her. Her apartment is empty."

Starr gave me an apologetic smile. "I'm sorry, I have to go. I don't really know anything." She rushed toward the car.

A short, stout woman bore down on me from the main building. "You be on your way, young man. You have no business here."

I blew out a breath. "I'm just looking for Lisa Oliver. I'm worried about her."

The woman propped a fist on each hip and glared at me. "If you were a good friend of Miss Oliver's, you'd know where she was. Now, be on your way."

I nodded. "Yes, ma'am. I'm sorry to have bothered you."

She held her bulldog stance until I drove away.

Three strikes and still no answers. I'd spent weeks trying to locate her. Then, when I had finally found her and managed to befriend her, she'd disappeared.

All my ideas exhausted, I headed back to the Bluebird Café. A busy place at dinnertime, but I didn't mind. I ordered the daily special. Roast beef and mashed potatoes with brown gravy, my favorite. After a leisurely meal, I headed back to my room planning to spend the rest of the evening sorting through boxes and deciding what to take with me.

Farrow's caution had haunted me throughout the day. *Be on your guard.*

How had he even known I was going to Tennessee? Had the FBI bugged my phone? I'd talked to Cran on the office phone, though. That would mean they were both bugged. That was the ultimate invasion of privacy.

His suggestion that I consider ditching the muscle car was not a new idea. I had thought about it several times. People always gave it a second look. If I pulled a late-night getaway like the Olivers, maybe I could leave it at Mom's and pick up a loaner. Mom was never home anyway. She was always caring for some patient or other. She wouldn't mind having my car in her garage a couple of days.

I pulled into the parking spot at my hotel. *Be on your guard.*

The power of suggestion messed with my mind. Every sound intensified as I walked toward the door. Was that a footstep? I sent a furtive glance over my shoulder. Nothing. Feeling a bit foolish, I shook my head and opened the door.

Before I could close it behind me, something like a battering ram slammed against the door, sending me flying backwards onto the corner of the bed. The door hit the wall as two men entered the room. With daylight behind them, they were only silhouettes, but I knew them.

The two dudes I'd met outside Asheville had found me. And Farrow had known they were coming.

The bigger guy grabbed a handful of my hair and pushed my head back. He pressed the cold barrel of a Colt Commander into my left temple and said, "Where is it?"

I had no idea what *it* was. "Where is what?"

He pushed harder. "You know what. Where's that stinking camera, boy?"

Camera? Why were they looking for my camera? Guy

number two was already tearing into the boxes and tossing my stuff everywhere.

I had to stop him. "My camera's not in those boxes. It's in the closet."

Guy number two leaped over the boxes and opened the closet door. He shook his head. "Don't see it."

Typical.

Gun guy loosened his grip on my hair and whacked me hard above my brow with the weapon. "Where is it?"

I blinked, trying to clear my mind. Then I eyed gun guy, waiting for an opportunity, hoping he'd take his attention off me. I only needed a few seconds. "It's on the floor."

He gestured to his partner. "Look on the floor."

I rolled out of gun guy's grasp, causing him to stumble forward. My jaw set, I zigzagged toward the door, any second expecting the crack of the gun followed by the pain of a bullet between my shoulder blades.

The gun fired as I zagged. A bullet zipped past my right ear lobe. As soon as I cleared the door, someone grabbed me around the chest and pulled me down.

"Stay down," Farrow rasped. "We've got them surrounded."

The cavalry had arrived. I swiped at the flow of blood

on my face from where the guy had slugged me and took deep breaths to keep from upchucking.

My next-door neighbor peeked through his curtains. I gave him a thumb's up to let him know I was okay.

Two black-clad agents escorted a handcuffed gun guy out of my room. Minutes later, a uniformed officer walked out and addressed Farrow.

"Petrov got away. He climbed out the bathroom window. My guys went after him."

Farrow blew out a breath and shook his head. Then he crouched in front of me and pressed a folded handkerchief against my brow. "You should probably get that looked at."

I have to admit, I was a little surprised by the concerned look on his face. "It's nothing. I've cut myself shaving and done more damage."

"Yeah, well, you could have a concussion."

"Are you going to tell me how you knew this was going down?"

Farrow stood. "Not here. Give me a minute. We'll sit inside."

I got up slowly, expecting dizziness or nausea. I had neither. Probably a good sign.

After the vehicles left, I sat down at my table.

Somehow, Farrow had found coffee.

He set a Styrofoam cup in front of me.

I took a sip and glanced around. My room looked like the aftermath of a tornado. Come to think of it, guy number two had been a bit like a whirlwind.

Farrow lowered himself into the chair opposite me. "I hate to admit it, but we had a mole problem."

"A mole? How did that happen?"

He shrugged. "The usual way. Cash was offered and accepted." He sipped his coffee. "Always disappointing, though."

I was processing. Had to be one of the two agents who had examined my car. Both had been standing nearby when Farrow asked me all those questions about what was usually in my trunk.

"I guess." Deep breath. "So, is it over? Supposing they catch Petrov, of course." They better catch him, otherwise, Lisa and I were still in jeopardy.

"Can't really say." He looked at me. "You know that. No details."

"It's not for an article."

"Doesn't matter. All I can tell you is this is bigger than those two goons."

STILL WATER

CHAPTER THIRTY-FOUR

Lisa

Allison's brother, Rick, swept me into a bear hug that pushed the air out of my lungs. He had put on some pounds since I'd seen him last, all muscle.

"Hi, Rick. It's been a while."

He released me but kept an arm around my shoulders. "I thought we'd seen the last of you. Went off to college and forgot all about us, didn't you?"

Before I could answer, Pop strode in. "Good to see you, son. Did you bring Hope with you?"

Rick removed his arm from my shoulder and stepped toward Pop. "We ran into Allison in town. Hope stayed with her. Apparently, they have some last-minute shopping to do."

"Oh, boy. More shopping." Pop winked at me. "This shindig is getting out of hand." He headed to the kitchen, where I heard him talking to Elsie.

After Pop left, Rick faced me again. "They tell you I'm getting married?"

I drew back. "You, too?"

He nodded. "In September, after we graduate and get settled. We met at school. She's a Lit major."

"I look forward to meeting her."

"You'll like her. She's beautiful, and she's smart like you."

I decided not to take offense at the first part of that remark. I smiled at him and shook my head. "So, what's she doing with you?"

His eyes widened, but he grinned. "She knows a good catch when she sees one."

I laughed. "Good comeback."

"Hey, I saw your little love bug in the driveway. One of the tires looks low. Toss me your keys and I'll take it to the shop out back and check it for you."

I crossed to the closet, found my key, and handed it over. "Just don't grind the gears."

He shook his head. "Like an elephant, you never forget, do ya?"

I faked a shocked look. "Did you just call me an elephant?"

"You're real funny, Oliver."

After being introduced to Hope, I stayed out of the way. The last couple of days, I had become quite attached to the swing by the lake. The tranquil spot quickly became my sanctuary. The water didn't bother me anymore. Maybe it was all that rest and relaxation.

When had I last slowed down this much?

Allison joined me. "I wondered where you went. I hope you aren't feeling you're in the way. You're not."

"I did wonder if I was sleeping in Hope's bed."

Allison chuckled. "No, she prefers a room of her own. She stays in Rick's room, and he camps out on the couch."

Maybe Hope wasn't as perfect as I had envisioned. "I've always heard men tend to marry women who look like their mothers." Hope certainly fit the pattern with her honey blond hair, green eyes and sparkling personality.

Allison toed the ground to keep the swing going. "Everyone says that about her. And they're right, in a way. But the likeness is skin deep." She glanced at me. "I like her. She's perfect for Rick. But she's an orchid among roses down here and she never lets us forget it."

There was no stopping the grin that followed that remark. Sometimes, sweet little Allison could be downright catty.

Allison giggled. "Don't get me wrong though, she's a lot of fun, and she'll be right in there with us, getting ready for the party."

That was the Allison I knew. Balancing her negative feelings with compliments and kind remarks. Admirable.

After supper, we all climbed into the car and headed to the Dairy Freeze. Aw, traditions. Maybe this really was my home.

Long after everyone had gone to bed, I lay staring at the ceiling, savoring each memory from the past few days. I was part of a family. Like a dry sponge, I had absorbed it all. I'd even enjoyed the prayer service on Wednesday night, and how the Pearls had anchored me in the middle of the row. Were they afraid I'd make a run for it?

Allison and I worked in the yard, weeding flowerbeds. I met the crazy kids who lived across the street. They answered all my questions about the old house until the eldest boy returned with a string of catfish he'd caught in Pop's lake.

The past few days almost made me forget my troubles. Almost. Snuggling down into the bed, I closed my eyes. I could sure get used to how quiet it was out this way.

I woke to the sound of laughter, probably coming from the kitchen. As usual, Allison's bed was already made. I squinted at the clock. Eight-fifteen. Since my teen years, I had always worked. Idleness was new to me, but Elsie kept telling me to rest. Still, I made a mental note to get up earlier and help Allison with her morning chores. Earn my keep. The phone rang as I padded toward the kitchen. Allison answered. From the sound of her voice, she was happy to hear from the caller.

"I'm so glad. We can't wait to see you. I will. Okay, drive carefully." She hung up as I entered the kitchen. "Ben's coming!"

"That's wonderful news," Elsie said. "What a blessing. All my children under one roof." She gave me a hug and a peck on the cheek. "Good morning, hon. I hope you slept well."

"I did." I looked at Allison. "Who's Ben?"

"My cousin. We thought he wasn't going to be able to come." She handed me an empty cup. "Coffee's ready."

Elsie hummed as she flipped pancakes.

The song was familiar, but I couldn't quite place it. I poured a cup of coffee and added cream. "Is everyone else still sleeping?"

Allison sat on a stool and cut into a stack of pancakes. "Rick's feeding the cows." She lowered her voice. "We won't see Hope for a while."

Elsie set a plate in front of me. "She needs her beauty sleep."

Blue skies greeted us on Saturday morning as we made the last-minute preparations for the afternoon barbecue.

"Break time," Elsie called from the back porch. "There are snacks in the kitchen, then let's rest for a while."

Elsie's "snack" was more than I usually ate in a day. If I kept eating like that, I'd grow out of my clothes.

After cleaning up, everyone sprawled around the living room, conversing, joking, and sharing favorite memories. I curled up in the corner of the sofa, content to observe from afar. More than anything, I wanted to memorize these moments and keep them forever in my heart.

I thought I heard a car door slam. Since no one reacted, I decided it must have been a neighbor.

Then the front door opened, but no one entered. The voices in the room stilled. My heart raced, I sat forward, straining to see if anyone would step inside.

I bit down hard on my lower lip. Had those two guys found me?

Allison jumped up. "Ben!" She dashed toward the door. "Ben's here."

Two disembodied arms folded around her. I heard a low, masculine chuckle as whoever it was lifted Allison off her feet.

Rick, Pop, and Elsie almost ran to the door.

Hope and I looked at each other.

Will laughed. "The prodigal son has returned."

I frowned. I'd had no idea there was a cousin, Ben. He must really be a black sheep, if they never even talked about him.

After the greetings on the porch, the group moved inside. The newcomer was the last to enter. When he did, my jaw sagged.

Jake.

Will and Hope rose to greet him, blocking my view. I took advantage of the momentary cover and slipped out of the room.

Panic ran races up and down my spine. I could not face him. Not yet. Maybe not ever. My feelings were still too raw.

CHAPTER THIRTY-FIVE

Jake

At first, I thought I was hallucinating. Lisa Oliver in Aunt Elsie and Pop's home? When I looked again, she was gone. I blinked my eyes. Disappeared, if she was ever there to begin with. For the moment, I concentrated on greeting Will and Hope.

Allison touched Hope's arm. "Where did Lisa go?"

I arched a brow, looking from one girl's face to the other. "Lisa, who?"

Allison started toward the kitchen. "Lisa Oliver."

I turned just in time to catch a pointed gaze from Aunt Elsie. *Uh-oh.*

Hands on her hips, she stood in front of me. "How do you know Lisa?"

I frowned. "How do you know I know her?"

"The look on her face when you walked through that door."

If Lisa had seen me and taken off, then something was amiss. I needed to find out what. "I, uh, we met in Lexington. We're friends."

Aunt Elsie kept giving me that look.

"I need to find her."

"Yes, you do. She's one of my kids, Ben, and a close friend to Allison. You'd better make things right."

I found Allison peering out the kitchen window. The gaze she turned on me held questions.

I spoke first. "Did you find her?"

"She's out on the dock. Care to tell me why she ran from you?"

"That's what I need to find out."

On the way to the lake, I mused over the possibilities. Lisa must have discovered why I'd been in Lexington. Either that, or she thought I had something to do with the break-in. I touched the wound above my brow, then tugged my hair forward to cover it.

Lisa sat on the edge of the dock, resting her chin on her knees. I could feel her misery from where I stood. I bowed my head and sighed. How do I get out of this one?

I'd known from the beginning how it would end.

I approached slowly. Didn't want to startle her.

She glanced over her shoulder but didn't move. That would have been reassuring, if not for the steely glint in her eyes.

"What are you doing here, Jake? And why did they call you Ben? Did you lie about that too?"

I lowered myself onto the dock beside her. At least now, I had a pretty good idea of why she didn't try to say goodbye. "I never lied to you, Lisa."

She drew back. "Right. I know you were using me to get information about my parents."

How had she found out about that?

"I never lied. You knew I was a reporter."

She clamped her fingers over the end of the dock, keeping her eyes on the water. Though she seemed calm, the exaggerated rise and fall of her shoulders revealed the turmoil of her emotions. She was seething.

I blew out a breath. "I didn't tell you everything, that's all."

"You withheld the facts about why you were in

Lexington." She leveled her gaze at me. "Omission is a form of lying."

I bowed my head and took a breath to control my emotions. "All right, I'll give you that. I apologize for having omitted the whole truth. But would you have talked to me if I'd been up front about who I was and why I'd followed you all the way to Lexington?"

Her lips twitched, but she didn't speak.

"That's what I thought. I know you're angry with me right now, Lisa, but give me ten minutes of your time. Hear me out, and then if you still don't want me around, I'll leave."

She turned her head to look at me. "Will you drop the story?"

"That'll be your choice."

No answer. Her gaze returned to the lake.

"I just happened to be at the police station the morning after the accident. I heard a couple of cops talking about it, so I decided to check it out."

I gave her the complete narrative, ending with Hamilton ordering me to tell the police what I'd learned. "For some reason, the local cops had called in the Feds. Agent Farrow."

A frown creased her brow. "Farrow? So, *you* were the

source."

It wasn't a question. She was connecting the dots.

I nodded confirmation. "I told them everything I'd overheard and gave them the photographs I'd taken, including the ones of the suspects' vehicle. The next day, I went to the cemetery."

She glared at me again. "I never saw you there."

"I knew it was a private service, so I . . . um, pretended to visit a nearby grave."

Her eyes widened. "That was you?"

"I thought you'd seen me, but I wasn't sure."

"But why, Jake?" Her expression hardened. "If that's really your name."

"Jacob Benjamin Bradley. My friends call me Jake. My family calls me Ben."

"Your family?"

"I told you about my family, remember? My aunt and uncle took me in. My cousins—"

"Rick and Allison are your cousins. The Pearls are your family."

Slow nod. Again, I wondered whether it was coincidence, or fate? Had God led me to her?

She reached for the railing and stood. "Then I should be the one to leave."

I jumped up. She was already walking away. "No, Lisa. You're just as much family as I am. Even more so. Allison will have my head on a platter if you leave."

If I read her expression correctly, she was considering the possibility of my head on a platter. At that moment, it was probably her preference. I steeled myself for her answer.

She leaned against the railing, drew a deep breath, and slowly exhaled before raising her eyes to mine. "I don't want to ruin Allison's day. This party means too much to her."

I rubbed the back of my neck. "So, can we get past this? Can you forgive me for withholding certain ... facts?" I stepped closer. "I really am sorry, Lisa."

"The worst part was, I was beginning to trust you. I don't—I've never done that."

I gripped the railing, keeping several feet between us. "I know. I'm even more sorry about that."

I turned to face her. "That day, at the cemetery, I caught a glimpse of your face. Something happened inside me. I can't really tell you what it was, but I had to know more about what happened. And about you." I found her gaze and held it. "I couldn't walk away. I couldn't forget about it. I kept seeing your face."

I still saw her face, every time I closed my eyes. But she would never understand that. She would probably think it was creepy. Maybe it was.

She straightened. "I need time, Jake. I need to think, on my own. Can you give me that?"

"Of course." *Just don't run,* I wanted to add, but I couldn't. Instead, I turned back to the water as she strode away.

Lisa

Ugh. Seeing Jake again shocked me, but having him so close . . . hearing what sounded like heartfelt words . . . I shook all over. I was surprised he didn't seem to notice the quiver in my voice. Everything about him drew me. I wanted to throw myself in his arms and let him comfort me.

Why was I so weak around him?

Nausea churned as I walked back to the house. I had to get to Allison's room unseen and find a quiet place to think. I suppose that conundrum could be the downside to having a family.

Everyone was in the kitchen, so I crept through the

side door and slipped down the hall. With Allison's bedroom door closed, I sat on the edge of the bed. My thoughts whirled like a dust devil, refusing to settle. I wanted to cry, but my eyes were dry. How could that be?

Allison peeked in. "It's just me." She stepped inside and closed the door behind her. Seconds later, she enveloped me in her arms.

I melted. I wept all the tears I had been holding inside.

Allison said nothing, just kept passing me tissues.

Finally, I sat back, pushed my hair away from my eyes and looked at her.

"Help me understand what's happening, Lisa. How do you know Ben?"

"We met in Lexington. I thought it was a chance meeting, but he was after a story." I looked at her. "About my parents."

She bit her lip and shook her head. "There's more to it than that. I saw how he looked at you."

I drew a breath. "Let me go back further." I glanced at the clock. Still two hours until the party.

She nodded. "We have time."

I told her everything that had happened back in Lexington, even the suspicions about my parents' deaths and the trashing of my apartment, but stopped short of telling her about the nightmares, how they had become more real. No need to go into all that.

And I didn't tell her how I felt about Jake. I could barely admit that to myself.

She took my hand. "You should let him help you. He's the best, Lisa. He's got a real talent for getting at the truth."

Let him help me? Maybe I could, if I wasn't so angry at him.

Elsie called from the hallway, "Allison, are you getting ready, hon?"

"Yes, we are, Mama. We'll be out soon."

As she stood and began changing her clothes, guilt washed over me. How could I be so selfish? "I'm sorry, I shouldn't have burdened you with all that, when you need to concentrate on your party."

"I'm glad you talked about it. You'll feel better now." She shrugged into a lacy slip before stepping into the bathroom.

Before I'd had time to compose myself, she was out again. "Your turn. Wash your face and put on a smile. Everything will turn out okay."

I grimaced. "You sound just like your mother."

"Not a bad thing, I hope," she called from inside her

closet.

"No, not at all."

CHAPTER THIRTY-SIX

Lisa

I ran the brush through my hair one more time and checked my makeup. My eyes were still a bit puffy. When had I become so self-absorbed?

When I opened the door and stepped into the hall, I nearly collided with Jake. Had he been waiting for me? I took a backward step.

Proud Jake no more, judging by his expression. More like a chastised puppy. I smiled at the thought.

He lowered his head and murmured, "I hope that smile is for me."

I gave him a sideways glance as I slid past him. "It is kind of."

He followed me. "I'll take *kind of*."

If only I'd had something else to wear besides my new red sundress. I walked into the kitchen and glanced around to see if there was something that needed to be done. My gaze stopped at Jake's admiring eyes.

I tried for a withering glance.

He answered with a bemused smile.

Ugh. I headed for the door, hoping to put space between us before I did something stupid.

Jake followed.

Would it be rude to let the screen door slam in his face?

He reached past me and pushed it open with a big paw.

I paused on the back porch steps, battling my emotions. I really needed to let go of the anger. One look at Allison deflated most of it. Dressed in a peasant-style cotton dress in her favorite shade of pink, a soft, rosy hue that perfectly matched the color of her cheeks, she was a shining light.

I could only admire her.

"Beautiful," Jake whispered.

I glanced up at him. Was he talking about Allison, or me? His eyes were on me. What I saw in them sent a shock wave through me so strong, I gripped the banister for support.

He stepped past me to join Will and Allison.

I made a beeline for Elsie.

Sensing my unease, she rested an arm at my waist. "Oh, don't you look lovely? Come and meet my friends."

Jake

I watched as Lisa attached herself to Aunt Elsie. Of course, she would choose a safe haven.

Pop put his hand on my shoulder. "Penny for your thoughts."

I shook my head at him. "I was thinking how I'd rather see Lisa mingling with friends rather than sticking like a burr to Aunt Elsie."

Pop stuck his hands in his pockets. "She's not ready. The girl's been through a lot these last few months."

He didn't know the half of it. "I know she has."

"You're fond of her, I think."

Not wanting to look at him, I examined my shoes. "It's obvious, huh?"

"Yep. Surprising, too."

I glanced up. "You don't think she's my type?"

"It's not that. You've always kept everyone in the dark about your feelings." He chuckled. "You must be mellowing with age."

I closed my eyes. He was right. "The first time I saw her, Pop, it's like she burrowed right into my heart. I can't shake it."

He looked me in the eye. "Why would you want to, son? Seems to me, you two need each other."

I shook my head. "She would not agree with you."

"So, you say." He grinned. "Give her time, Ben. She's wounded."

Time. Isn't that what I'd been doing? "I suppose you're right."

Pop moved away, leaving me alone with my thoughts. I leaned against the smooth bark of a young maple tree. A power stronger than myself had led me to this point. For what reason? The story was about to be shelved, but the need to know ran stronger than ever through my veins. I couldn't lay it down.

What if she asked me to let the story go?

Could I let it go? Let her go? Why would God bring her into my life, only to take her away?

My gaze found Lisa again. She was laughing at Pop, who was probably sharing one of his silly jokes. I pushed away from the tree and strolled toward a group of friends gathered near the buffet table.

A familiar voice piped up. "Hey, Bradley, long time no see!"

I turned to greet an old baseball buddy. This party for Allison and Will deserved my full attention, or at least as much attention as I could part with.

Lisa

Allison, Hope, and I had helped Elsie wash the dishes and clean the kitchen. The guys were still outside, cleaning up the yard.

Elsie dried her hands on a dish towel. "You girls pour yourselves something to drink and sit down to rest."

Hope carried a glass of soda to the kitchen table and sank into the nearest chair with a loud sigh. "It was a wonderful party, Mama Pearl."

"Ya'll all helped. I couldn't have done it without you. But I appreciate the compliment, darlin'."

Allison handed me an ice-cold coke. I smiled my thanks. She knew me well. I sat across from Hope. Moments later, Allison joined us.

Hope looked at her. "You're going to have to set a date now, you know."

Allison nodded. "I know. It's just so hard, not knowing when our house will be finished."

Elsie set a platter of ham and cheese sandwiches in the center of the table. "They want to have the house ready first. We told them they could stay here, but they weren't having it."

The sound of masculine laughter and heavy footsteps on the back porch brought an end to the conversation. The door opened and Pop entered, followed by Rick, Will, and Jake.

I had hoped Jake would leave after the party. Not because I didn't want to see him. I did. That was the problem.

The guys joined us at the big kitchen table and grabbed sandwiches while Elsie poured their drinks.

After making the first round, Elsie frowned at me. "Where's your sandwich? You need to eat, too."

I shook my head. "I'm not hungry."

Pop chuckled. "I bet she'd eat another piece of that cake if you offered."

I bit my lip to keep from smiling. I had just been thinking the same thing.

Hope leaned forward. "What a lovely locket, Lisa. Does it open?"

I gripped the locket and pressed the release. "Yes, it does. My parents gave it to me, before they . . ." I bowed my head. When I looked up, Jake's eyes were on me. He didn't add to the conversation, but I couldn't help wondering what was going on in that quick mind of his.

Elsie stepped behind me. "What lovely photos. Look how young they were. I know you treasure those."

I nodded.

"May I see?" Allison asked.

I slipped the necklace over my head and handed it to her. The rings jangled against the heart as she lowered it to the table. Her eyes found mine. "Are those—?"

I nodded. "Their wedding rings."

Hope looked at the photos next and then passed the necklace back to me.

I avoided Jake's gaze as I returned it to my neck. I could almost see his fingers twitching to get hold of those pictures. My parents had avoided cameras like the plague, so these were the only photos of them. I clicked the locket shut and fastened the chain around my neck.

After everyone had a piece of cake, Hope headed to her room.

Pop and Elsie were the next ones to call it a night.

When Will stood up to leave, Allison followed. "I'll see you out."

The grandfather clock in the den chimed ten times. It seemed much later.

Rick elbowed Jake. "What's your plan, man? You staying the night?"

I sneaked a peek at Jake.

He was looking at me. "I'm in town for a few days."

Rick stretched his arms over his head. "Okay. Well, I'm turning in. See you folks in the morning." He gathered the bottles and carried them to the back porch before heading back through the kitchen.

With one last look at me, Jake stood. "Goodnight, Lisa."

Since Rick was still in the room, I couldn't avoid answering. "Goodnight."

Jake left through the back door. I waited but didn't hear the thrum of the Camaro's engine.

I was still sitting at the table when Allison popped back in. Her warm smile helped fill the emptiness left by Jake.

"We better go to bed. Mama will have us up early to get ready for church."

I followed her to our room, still wondering where Jake had gone, but I was not about to ask.

"What a lovely day we had," Allison whispered as she snuggled into her bed. "Thanks for all your help."

"I didn't do that much."

"Oh, yes you did. I've loved having you here." She yawned. "You and Ben."

I froze. What did she mean by that?

"I get to spend the next few days with two of my favorite people."

STILL WATER

CHAPTER THIRTY-SEVEN

Lisa

I wasn't sure how Jake managed to sit beside me in church. Especially since I'd taken such care to sandwich myself in between Elsie and Allison. The next thing I knew, Allison was waving Jake over. I glared at her, but she ignored me.

To make things worse, we were all crowded into a single pew, so it was almost impossible not to touch the person next to you. I tried to keep my mind on the proceedings. Good thing I'd brought my new notebook and a pen.

As the pastor began his sermon, I jotted down the reference, Ephesians 4:32.

"... and be ye kind to one another, tenderhearted,

forgiving one another, even as God for Christ's sake hath forgiven you."

The pastor gripped the sides of the podium as he leaned forward. "Can you forgive that one who wronged you?"

I lifted my eyes to his face, as though he spoke only to me. These men of God seemed able to read my thoughts. It was uncanny.

Jake had asked my forgiveness, and I had ignored his request. I had behaved badly. I didn't understand why, but every thought of him brought pain, like a knife in my heart. I laid my pen down and fingered the locket.

"When you've been hurt, it's easy to hold onto the pain and store it up," the pastor continued. "It sours like old milk. Before you know it, you're carrying bitterness in your heart."

I didn't want to become bitter. I could easily let go of what Jake had done. I could forgive him, though it meant I'd have to talk to him. Something deeper and darker hid in my heart. I'd need to deal with that, too.

My parents.

Jake

When Pastor Hadley's sermon ended and the congregation stood for the closing hymn, I realized I hadn't heard a word he'd said.

Lisa sat ramrod stiff throughout. At one point, I thought she was going to take notes, but she stopped at the opening Scripture.

As we filed out of the pew, I spied Lou Anne Tate and quickly ducked my head. We had briefly dated my junior year of high school. Ever since then, she had considered me the one that got away and seemed determined to gain a second chance whenever I was in town.

I turned and caught Lisa by the arm. "Lisa, there you are."

Her eyes widened.

I lowered my voice. "May I escort you out? Big favor. I'm begging." I winked. Why had I done that?

She gave me a searing glare but allowed me to guide her toward the door. "I will expect an explanation."

"You'll get one."

Lou Anne's eagle eye caught me. Oh no.

She trampled two old ladies trying to get to us. "Ben Bradley, I didn't know you were in town. How on earth are you?"

"Why, hello, Lou Anne."

Her gaze locked onto the girl attached to my arm. "And who is this?"

I smiled at Lisa. "This is, uh, Lisa Oliver, my, uh—"

Lisa interrupted my stumbling intro by offering her hand to Lou Anne. "It's a pleasure to meet you."

Lou Anne's gray eyes frosted over. "Nice to meet you, too. How long have you known Ben?"

Lisa fake-smiled at me. "We met in May."

"Well, that's a long time for you, Ben, I'm impressed." She eyed Lisa again. "I've known Ben for a long, long time. He moves around a lot." She winked. "If you know what I mean."

Before either of us could respond, Allison called from the doorway, "Ben, Lisa, time to go!"

I nodded to Lou Anne. "Nice to see you again." I grabbed hold of Lisa's hand. She almost had to run to keep up with me.

Will's car waited at the curb. Allison sat up front, so I held the door for Lisa, then trotted around to the other side. I was barely in when Will took off.

He chuckled as he gunned the accelerator. "Whew! That was a close one, buddy. Lou Lou almost got her claws into you again."

Allison giggled. "Sorry about that, Lisa. We should have warned you."

Lisa shot a glance in my direction. "Someone should have."

I cleared my throat. "Yeah, thanks for your help."

She folded her hands in her lap and tossed a coy smile my way. "So, fearless Jake, have I found your Achilles heel?"

Will and Allison's laughter delayed my response. I spent those moments trying to construct a witty reply, but when Lisa reached for my hand, my mind turned to mush.

She spoke in a low voice, "Will you forgive me for the way I treated you?"

I blew out a breath. Wow. "Of course." Was she going to elaborate? We stared at each other for an extended interval, but she didn't explain any further.

She glanced down at my hand that she was still holding and let go.

My palm felt strangely empty. I looked out the window. We were less than a mile from the house. A good thing.

Aunt Elsie's jaw nearly hit the floor. "Oh, my word!"

I figured she would be excited when I told her about my column's popularity, but I hadn't expected the jig she danced before she tried to squeeze the stuffing out of me.

Allison joined in the hug. "Why didn't you tell us, you big lug?"

I kissed her cheek. "Yesterday was all about you, kid."

"Don't forget me, buddy," Will said. "My day, too." He put his arm around Allison's waist and pulled her toward him. "Every bride's gotta have a groom."

I smacked a kiss on my fingertips and pressed them against Will's cheek. "There you go. Didn't mean to leave you out, man."

Will swiped at his cheek. "Gross!"

A sweet sound came to me from across the room. I turned to find Lisa laughing out loud at my joke.

Pop shook my hand. "Proud of you, son."

High praise from Pop.

Since Rick and Hope had gone, Aunt Elsie urged me to move my stuff from the room above the shop into Rick's room.

Even though it was Sunday, Allison had already changed the bed linens. I could get used to this kind of service.

Rick's room was right across the hall from a small den that housed a sleeper sofa, two overstuffed chairs, and a television set. It was a quiet room clad in walnut paneling. A single window allowed an expansive view of the driveway and the intersection of Church Road and Sundrop Lane. Surveillance-wise, it was not as good as the old rec room above the shop. I was closer to the family here though, so I couldn't complain.

I sat on the sofa and leaned forward, staring at the floor. This had always been my safe place. My home, my family since childhood. I rested my head in my hands. If I had exposed them to danger—how could I live with that?

STILL WATER

CHAPTER THIRTY-EIGHT

Jake

A tap at the door interrupted the best sleep I'd had in days. I rolled over and squinted into the semidarkness. The odd silhouette cleared up when I switched on the bedside lamp. Aunt Elsie, with her hair still done up in bobby pins.

"Your friend, Lieutenant Roberts, is on the phone for you."

I sat up and swung my legs over the side of the bed. Good thing I'd borrowed some of Rick's old pj's. I ran my fingers through my hair and tugged some down in front to cover the injury. "I'll take it in the den."

"All right but try not to wake the girls. They're still sleeping." She turned on a lamp in the den and closed the door after I'd picked up the phone.

"Hello?"

"Sorry to call so early, man, but you know our workday has already started up here."

A click on the line told me Aunt Elsie had hung up the kitchen extension.

"Right. Mine normally would have. What's up?"

"There was a manila envelope waiting for me when I arrived at the office, delivered by courier from an unidentified source."

I knew the source, but I couldn't tell Cran. The less said about it, the better. "Containing?"

"More than you bargained on, I'll bet. Not good news for the daughter, I'm afraid."

I sat in the armchair and leaned forward. "What is it?"

"Oliver was running drugs on the east coast—for someone big, apparently. He was picked up by the authorities back in February. Sat in jail for a couple of days, until he agreed to a deal."

I winced. Then I glanced around me to be sure I was alone. "Drugs? No, man. Are you sure about that?"

"I have the report right here. Oliver turned in some good intel, but the Feds needed more. They gave him a camera and asked for proof. I did some checking of my own as well. This is legit." Cran was nothing if not thorough.

"That's why they were after him."

"Somehow, those drug runners caught on to him. They were after the film."

By the time Cran had finished, I had a ball of tension between my shoulder blades. "This is bad."

"I agree."

I stood and moved to the window. "Can I get a copy of that report?"

"I'll send it to you today, but I'm going to have to redact the identifiers. We don't want this to fall into the wrong hands. Where should I send it?"

"I'll be here until the weekend, but maybe it would be better to send it to my temporary office, care of Albert Russell. I'll call and let him know to expect it."

"Sounds good. Next time you head my way, you can pick up the original. You're going to need it if you intend to proceed."

"Hamilton pulled the plug on the story but advised me to keep him in the loop."

"Yeah, he knows you almost as well as I do. I'll let you go. Call if you need anything."

"Will do. Thanks, Cran." I hung up the phone. Staring

out the window, I rubbed the back of my neck, hoping to release some of the tension already building. Too early for this much stress. A glance at the grandfather clock above the television told me it was barely six-thirty.

Cran had been putting in extra hours trying to keep up with his work and my research. I owed him big time.

I shot across the hall to my room. I could well imagine the teasing I'd get over the pajamas I was wearing. Besides being 1960s-ugly, the pants were high waters.

While I showered and shaved, I mentally processed what Cran had shared. Bill Oliver had been transporting drugs, most likely heroin, which explained a lot. Particularly how a truck driver and a waitress could pay cash for college. I sent up a quick prayer that Lisa would never hear about that.

I had promised her I wouldn't withhold information, but how could I tell her this, especially now? The truth was certain to come out at some point. By that time, though, maybe she would be in a better position to handle it.

And then there was the film. That had to be what the guys were looking for in my room when they wanted my camera. The photos Bill Oliver had taken had sealed his fate. I believe he knew he was driving toward his death.

I halfway suspected he had driven off that road on

purpose.

I shrugged into a dark blue tee and strode toward the front of the house.

Aunt Elsie's kitchen welcomed me like an old friend. She sat at the table, working on a crossword puzzle. Minus the bobby pins, her hair stood in springy curls, waiting for her to brush them into submission.

She looked up when I entered. "Coffee's ready, hon. Pour yourself a cup and come help me with this puzzle. I'm stuck."

I grinned as I poured the steaming, hot liquid into a mug. It was great to be home. "What's the clue?"

She tilted her head to the side. "British land measure?"

I sat down next to her and peered at the puzzle. "Seven letters, beginning with an r? I think you have four-down wrong, because the land measure is hectare."

"Oh." She erased the wrong letters and filled in the answer for ten across. "Thanks."

"Is everyone sleeping late?"

She shook her head. "The girls are seeing to the chickens." She set her pencil down, picked up her cup, and took a sip. "So, Lieutenant Roberts calling so early, does it have something to do with our girl?"

"Our girl?" I shook my head and smiled. With her eagle eyes focused on my face, I couldn't lie. But I could deflect. "It's Mr. Roberts now. Cran resigned active duty."

"Uh-huh. I know. You didn't answer my question. Does it have something to do with . . . our former neighbors?"

"I can't really talk about it. Not yet." Maybe never.

She sighed. "Well, no one likes to hear unpleasantness about their loved ones." She patted my arm. "You know all about that."

I looked at her. "Yes, I do." I laid my hand over hers as I sipped my coffee.

A slight frown creased her brow. "That girl—she's had such a tough time."

I knew she would never try to get me to talk about something that wasn't her business. Lisa was her immediate concern. That was her way, always looking after her *kids*.

"Just pray for me. I don't really know how to handle this one."

"I'll be happy to do that." She gave my hand a squeeze, then rose from the table. "Right now, though, I'd better get breakfast going."

I downed the rest of my coffee and stood. "I think I'll

take a walk and clear my head."

"Good idea." She set the skillet on a burner. "Just don't be late for breakfast." She pointed a spatula at me. "And don't think I haven't noticed that bruise on your noggin. Is there anything I need to know about that?"

I couldn't stop the grin as I bent to press a kiss against her cheek. "Nope. You don't need to know."

Lisa

The setting sun cast a golden glow over Pop's lake. Allison and I reclined on a quilt just below the swing where Pop and Elsie sat.

Allison thumbed through a bridal magazine, thick with notes and tabbed pages.

At first, I tried to "ooo" and "ah" at the right moments, but soon realized it didn't matter. She was in her own world.

Pop sighed. "Evenings like this one always remind me of my favorite psalm. He began to quote from memory the twenty-third psalm. "The Lord is my shepherd; I shall not want . . ."

The words flowed over me like liquid peace. This time,

I really listened.

"He leadeth me beside the still waters . . ."

As the words pierced my heart, my vision blurred. Dark pines. Smooth, black water. Someone calling my name. I struggled for air.

"Lisa?" Allison's touch on my arm brought me back. "Are you all right?"

I drew a slow, cleansing breath before nodding. "I'm fine." A quick glance told me Pop and Elsie hadn't noticed.

Pop continued, "Yea, though I walk through the valley of the shadow of death, I will fear no evil . . ."

I will fear no evil. God is with me.

Allison was watching me.

I tried to lighten up. "I'm fine, really."

Hearing voices, I looked up to see Will and Jake approaching. They had gone to return the car Jake had borrowed, which puzzled me. Where was his Camaro and how was he planning to get back home?

Allison patted my hand. "You sure you're okay?"

I sensed Jake's eyes on me. I kept mine front and center. "Yes. I'm fine."

Will sat beside Allison. "Hello, beautiful."

Elsie halted the swing. "How was your mother, Ben?"

Jake crouched next to her. "She's well. Busy, as

usual."

Pop stood. "Well, it's time for me to head that way. I'll see you gals and fellas sometime tomorrow."

I watched as he and Elsie strolled, hand-in-hand, toward the house, another scene I meant to hold in my memories.

Jake moved closer and sat on the ground beside me. "You're heading back on Saturday morning, right?"

I glanced at him. "Yes."

"Can I bum a ride to Lexington?"

Wild thoughts and possible reactions chased themselves through my mind, but in the end, I could not say no. "Sure. I guess."

He grinned. "You guess?"

I forced myself to look at him. "Of course. I can take you." Heat flooded my cheeks. I was never going to be good at this interaction stuff.

He leaned close. "I promise I'll behave."

STILL WATER

CHAPTER THIRTY-NINE

Lisa

This morning, I wrote in my journal for the first time in over a week.

> *Even though life is much slower in the country, the days seem to pass at the speed of light. Must be because I don't want them to.*

I had barely seen Jake, except at mealtimes. He spent most of his time either on the phone or working around the farm. And in truth, I'd been avoiding him. He hadn't seemed to object. Why did that bother me so much?

I was packing when the phone rang.

I heard Elsie's voice in the hall. "Ben, there's an Agent

Farrow on the phone for you."

Agent Farrow? I dropped the blouse I was folding and stepped to the doorway.

"I'll get it back here," Jake said.

I ducked back into the room. When I heard his voice on the phone, I checked the hall. It was empty, so I tiptoed to the open door of the den where he stood with his back to me. I moved out of sight, but still within hearing.

"I'm just fine, how are you?"

Pleasantries, like they were old friends. I hesitated. It was wrong to eavesdrop, but I couldn't seem to move.

"Yes, I've seen her. She's safe. No need to worry."

He had to be talking about me. I bit my lip. I had made Jake promise to be honest with me and here I was, sneaking around behind his back.

"I'll be in town sometime late tomorrow."

I stepped into the doorway. May as well make my presence known.

Jake chuckled. "True. She won't like confinement, but you're right. It's best this way."

What? Confinement. No. Just no. I would not—

At that moment, Jake turned, and I froze as his eyes met mine. His lips curved into a smile. When I started to duck away, he held up his hand as if he wanted me to wait.

"Sure, I'll give you a call then." He hung up the phone, still holding my gaze. "That was Agent Farrow. He wants a meeting with me when I return."

I folded my arms over my chest. "What did he mean by confinement? Was he talking about me?"

"What? Oh." He frowned and shook his head. "No, not you, my car. Back in Lexington, he suggested I find another set of wheels. My Camaro is too high profile. Turns out, he was right. I left it in Mom's garage so it's out of the way." He ran his fingers through his hair.

"Oh." My turn to frown. Why was his forehead yellow? Curious, I stepped closer. "Is that a bruise?"

He turned away from me briefly to stuff some papers into his duffel. "There's something we need to discuss."

I opened my mouth to tell him I wasn't ready. I hadn't made a decision yet.

He read my expression and shook his head. "Not about us, or rather, not about me. Do you want to sit?" He indicated the sofa.

My eyes on his forehead, I lowered myself onto the couch, fighting the urge to lift his hair and get a look at that bruise.

He sat across from me, conveniently out of reach of my itching fingers. "I talked to a buddy of mine this morning. Crandall Roberts. We served together in the Navy. We now know why the FBI is involved."

I sat forward. "Why?"

He took a breath and exhaled.

In those few seconds, a river of panic broke loose inside me. My pulse quickened. I held up my hand. "Wait. I'm not sure I want to know."

He reached for my hand and held it. "It's all right, Lisa. As it turns out, your dad was trying to help the Feds." He shrugged. "Apparently, he'd gotten into a little trouble. Maybe not of his own doing, we're not sure. That's one of the things I'd like to find out. So, he got mixed up with the wrong people. He was then approached by an undercover agent and offered leniency if he would help them get evidence."

All the air left my lungs as I sat back, pulling my hand from his grasp. I'd known something was wrong. I'd felt it. "When was that?"

He shook his head. "Not sure of the exact date. Early spring, maybe?"

I fingered the locket. Dad had been away longer than normal. The last time I had talked to Mom, she'd mentioned it. She never did that, so I'd known she was worried.

Jake eyed the locket a moment before bringing his attention back to my face. "They gave your dad a small camera and asked him to take some photos. And he did. He had the film concealed in a coffee thermos when he ran off the road. It was washed downstream. Thankfully, the Feds found it before anyone else did."

"So, that's what they were after? A roll of film?" And that was why they had cut up my belongings. But, if they were after a roll of film, why had Farrow asked for Dad's watch?

Jake sat forward, elbows on his knees, and looked at me. "Farrow told me, those two guys—you know, the ones they were looking for—they caught one of them. He's been arrested. The other one will be, soon. They'll be going away for a while. Probably a long while. Burglary, wanton endangerment, breaking and entering, and involuntary manslaughter, among other charges."

Arrested. One. There was still one out there. I bit down on my lip to stop its trembling.

"It's okay. We're safe. For now."

I met his gaze. "We?" Before he could stop me, I lifted my hand and swept his hair aside. It was worse than I'd expected, not just a bruise, but an ugly gash. "They did this?"

He took hold of my hand and held it between both of his. An impish grin transformed the seriousness of his expression. "Actually, Farrow did that. He put me in harm's way. Used me as bait."

"Farrow?"

He nodded. "Granted, I would have volunteered if he'd given me the chance. But there was a reason he wanted to keep me in the dark."

I pulled my hand from his grasp. "Why would he do that?" My parents were already dead. Jake was hurt and could have been killed. "This has to stop." I stood and headed for the door.

Jake

Now, what was she upset about? When Lisa shot from the room like a cannonball, I was right behind her. My steps slowed at the outside door. Maybe she needed a few minutes to calm down. I could give her that. Besides, I knew where she was headed.

The sun sparkled on the surface of the lake. Lisa stood in silhouette against it. I stepped onto the dock and squinted into the blue sky overhead. "It is so peaceful out here."

She faced me. "I don't know if I want you to dig into their past. What if—"

I watched the changes in her face as I waited for her to finish. Shadows and light. Doubt, or was it fear? What was she so afraid of?

"Mom's last words—that they'd left to protect me— I'm not completely sure what that meant. Protect me from what or who? Is that why Dad taught me self-defense? To protect me from someone?"

She was working it out in her mind, not really expecting an answer from me. But I'd been giving a lot of thought to the way she'd been raised. "Maybe he wasn't so much teaching you to protect yourself. He was instilling confidence. He wanted you to be self-sufficient." Looking at her now, I wasn't so sure her dad had been successful.

She was silent for several minutes and as still as the water she watched. "As long as I can remember, I've had a recurring dream, a nightmare. Dark, green water surrounded by big trees. I think they're evergreens, because I can almost smell the pine. And then I see something white floating on the water, bobbing up and down. I move toward it, curious."

Her eyes held a faraway look, as though she was

reliving the dream. I stepped closer.

She twisted her hands together. "It was a body. A dead body."

Now, she had my interest. "Do you know who it was?"

She shook her head. "No. The dream always ends there. Sometimes, I wake myself up before I get too close. Lately, I've been wondering if it's something that really happened. A trauma in my life." She turned back to the water. "That's why I don't know if I want to know."

"Wait." I parked myself next to her. "You think this thing really happened, and your parents were somehow involved?" I took her hands in mine. "Lisa, it could just be a dream."

She looked into my eyes. "You don't know that. Why does it keep happening? What if it was real and they . . ."

She couldn't speak the words.

I mulled it over. She knew her parents better than anyone, which made her suspicions all the more credible.

The Olivers involved in a murder? After what I'd just heard from Cran, it was completely within the realm of possibility.

CHAPTER FORTY

Lisa

I couldn't keep running away. At some point, I had to find home. I had to trust someone. My eyes found Jake's. He cared about me. I could see it on his face and in every move he made.

But.

Why is there always an addendum with me? A negative contraction followed by ten reasons why I should not or could not do whatever it was I wanted to do.

It always came back to my upbringing and the two people I had relied on most of my life. Now, I even doubted them.

It wasn't Jake's fault. Not really. He was doing his job. He had said he couldn't walk away. It was more than a story to him, it was personal.

There were some big hurdles out there for me, all of them labeled with a different name, but all coming down to one—fear. I was afraid of what Jake might find.

Who were my parents, really? Were they on the run from an ugly past? I closed my eyes and bowed my head. There were too many unanswered questions.

Jake waited, a little apart, giving me space. It was something he'd done several times. He looked up when I stepped nearer. His shoulders slouched a little.

At ease, or disappointed? Judging by the look in his eyes, the latter was likely true. Had he given up on me?

I took another step. "I'm sorry, Jake, I'm not usually such a basket case."

"Comes with the territory. You're handling pretty well for what you've been through."

We stood side-by-side, looking at the pristine lake. The water was still and silent, mirroring the bright, blue sky.

I took a breath, gathering courage. "What do I need to do, Jake? How can I find out more about them?"

He lowered his head toward mine, his eyes searching, probing. "You mean it?"

I nodded. "I'm still . . . afraid of what you may find,

but yes, if there are answers out there, I want to know."

He drew a breath and released it. "Wow, I don't know what to say."

"Well, that's a first."

He quirked a smile. "It is rare for me."

"What happens now?"

"Would it be all right—could I see your locket?"

Since we stood so close to the water, I didn't want to remove the necklace and take a chance on dropping it. I opened it so he could see the photos.

He took the open heart in his fingers and examined its contents. "They look like teenagers."

Oh, how I wish his nearness had no effect on me. My hands were visibly shaking. I gripped the railing as I forced a calm response. "They may have been. I'm not sure when those photos were taken."

He snapped the locket closed and let it go. "I have an idea if you wouldn't mind. There's a camera shop in town. I know the owner. I think he can copy those and may be able to enlarge them a little. If it's okay with you."

"Is it safe? They're all I have."

He nodded. "It's perfectly safe, but we need to go now. He may need time to work on it."

Allison met us at the back door. "I was just on my way

to find you two. I have to go to town. Do you need anything?"

Jake and I exchanged looks.

He stood aside for me to enter ahead of him. "Can we tag along? I want to see if Mac can enlarge those photos of Lisa's parents."

Allison nodded. "I'm sure he can. I'll drop you off."

Mac's Camera Shop was small and centrally located on Main Street in Columbia. The owner greeted *Ben* with gusto. I hung back until Jake introduced us. As he explained our reason for stopping in, I removed the necklace and placed it on the glass counter.

Mac peered at the photos. "I can sure try." He glanced at me. "They'll be a little fuzzy, depending on how large you want the duplicates."

"We won't need them too much larger," Jake told him. "And make a couple copies of each."

Mac reached in a drawer and pulled out a pair of tweezers. "Let's get those out." He carefully removed Mom's photo and laid it aside. As he released the photo, it flipped over.

I noticed something written on the back and picked it up.

Jake leaned close. "What is it?"

"Writing—looks like "Water."

Mac turned the other one over. "This one says, "Still."

Jake slid the two pieces side-by-side. "Still Water?"

"Might be a place," Mac said. "Usually, folks write where the photo was taken, and sometimes the date."

Mom had told me that she cut the faces from her original photo to fit into the two sides of the locket. I looked at Jake. "Does that help at all?"

He shrugged. "It might. I'm sure there are lots of places known as Still Water, though."

"There's a Stillwater, Oklahoma," Mac said. He placed the photo cutouts in a small tray and wrote "Ben Bradley" on a card. "I reckon I can get this done pretty quick. I'll give you a call in the morning. You staying in Cully?"

Jake nodded. "Yes, you can call me there. Thanks, Mac."

Jake stepped out of the camera shop ahead of me and held the door. I glanced at his face as I passed. He didn't meet my eyes, but scanned the immediate vicinity, kind of like Dad used to do. An odd feeling passed over me, like creepy-crawlies.

He walked street-side next to me, always keeping me on the inside next to the buildings, also like Dad. Maybe it was a guy-thing.

We were supposed to meet Allison at the drug store, about two blocks from the camera shop. We'd gone nearly halfway when a loud bang sounded.

Before I had time to react, Jake had stepped in front of me and pressed me against the wall of the nearest building, using his body as a shield.

When an old box truck passed by, he released his hold on me and backed away. The truck backfired again before turning onto an adjoining street.

Jake shook his head. "Sorry, I . . ."

My back to the wall, I kept my eyes on him. "No, it's all right." Had he just tried to protect me from what he thought was a gunshot? I stood still, watching him.

He tilted his head, giving me a sideways look. "Are you okay?"

I swallowed. *No.* This man was ready to take a bullet for me. I forced my lips into a smile and gave him an affirmative nod. But I was not okay.

His eyes locked onto mine. "You're sure?"

"I'm fine. Just surprised."

He bowed his head. "Yeah, me too. I guess I'm a little

on edge." He touched my arm, urging me forward. "We better get going."

As I fell into step beside him, my mind reeled. Just like that, he had won my whole heart. How would I get through this next year when all I wanted was to be with this man? Every second.

Breathe, Lisa, breathe and think. This was not the time for frivolous pursuits. I had two more semesters to complete. Not just get through it but excel.

I owed it to Mom. I could not let myself get too involved with Jake right now. I sneaked a peek at him. He was still on high alert, scanning the surrounding area.

When we found Allison's car, Jake leaned against the front fender and crossed his arms over his chest.

Guarded. Powerful.

Uneasy, that was me. I stood next to him, trying to figure out how to say what was on my heart.

He broke the silence first. "Looking forward to getting back to school?"

"In a way." I met his gaze briefly and then averted my eyes. I couldn't say what I needed to say if I looked at him. "When I'm at school, I—I'm all in. The classes, the studying, consumes me. I want that. I need to excel." I glanced at him again. I could almost read the questions forming in his mind, so I rushed on.

"I can't have distractions." I shook my head. "No distractions. I owe it to her. To do my best."

"You owe it to whom?"

I lifted my eyes to his. "Mom. She sacrificed so much. She wanted me to finish free and clear, with no debt. I have to do my best. So, I can't have . . . distractions."

He laid his hand on my arm. "You keep saying that, Lisa. What is this distraction you're referring to?"

Where was Allison? This would be the perfect time for her to arrive before I made a complete fool of myself. When I shifted from one foot to the other, my purse strap slid off my shoulder. I grabbed for it.

Jake chuckled. He stood, towering over me. "You know I'm a facts person, Lisa. I need to understand. Are you referring to me? Am I the distraction?"

I bit my lip but gave no answer. I could not bring myself to meet his gaze. Even when a breeze blew hair into my eyes, I didn't make a move.

"Okay, I'll take that as a *yes*. So, the fact that I'm a distraction, while oddly flattering, is easily dealt with, Lisa. I'm not going to be in your way. I'll be pretty busy myself, these next few months." He stepped nearer to brush the hair from my eyes. "I must admit though, your confessed distraction gives me hope."

I looked at him. What did he mean by that?

He smiled, and for a brief instant, I thought he would kiss me. Instead, he backed away.

"I know how important this year is to you, Lisa. I've been there." He looked up, his eyes scanning again. "Where is Allison?"

For some reason, I laid my hand on his wrist. "I'll go check."

He nodded but made no reply, which did not surprise me. He had a lot to think about. Was it selfish of me to push him away, just when things were beginning to heat up between us?

I stepped through the rear entrance door of the shop and breathed in the cool air. Allison's voice sounded from somewhere in the front of the store. She had probably been waylaid by a friend.

As I stepped forward, a hand clamped over my mouth. A thick, hairy arm encircled my waist like a vise, pinning my arms against me. All my training over the years disappeared from my mind. I had no idea what to do or how to react. I wrenched myself and tried to scream.

He clamped down harder on my mouth.

I lost my footing as he dragged me backward toward

the door I had just entered. Had he been waiting for me? Would Jake see us and come to my rescue? Determined not to panic, I pulled air in through my nose and blinked back tears. What was it Dad used to say?

Fear kindles adrenaline. Let it make you strong.

I gritted my teeth and fought my attacker to no avail as he dragged me down the steps, staying within the shadows close to the back of the building. One thing came to mind—a last-ditch effort—and I had only moments to respond.

CHAPTER FORTY-ONE

Jake

Lisa had only been gone moments when the back door opened again and a man backed out, grappling with someone.

Lisa! I shot forward.

She struggled hard against him, keeping his attention on her and away from me as I sprinted toward them. I reached them as the man took his hand from her mouth to open a car door. His backward glance sent me into overdrive.

It was Petrov.

At that moment, Lisa doubled over, taking him by surprise. He fumbled to keep her in his grasp.

I looped my right arm over his head and around his

neck, grabbed my right wrist with my left hand, tightening my hold like a vise to cut off his breath. Then I dragged him away from the vehicle and Lisa.

Loosed from his grip, Lisa fell forward and rolled away then jumped up and ran.

Good girl!

Like an angered wolverine, Petrov turned on me, knocking us both to the ground. Unfortunately, I was on my back with a wriggling Petrov on top, his back to me. I kept my arms around his neck in a stranglehold, pressed my feet into the pavement, and tried to roll us over.

His teeth sank into my forearm.

I managed to roll most of the way over and used my body to hold him down.

A siren screamed nearby, sending Petrov into more of a frenzy. I had nearly lost my hold on him when Lisa dropped onto his legs and sat there. Her presence energized me. I pressed him to the ground so hard, he gave a loud groan.

Two uniformed police officers ran up and helped hold Petrov down.

"We have him," one of them told me. "You and the girl need to step aside and let us do our job."

I rolled off Petrov and pushed up from the ground.

Lisa fell into my arms, sobbing. I held her as tremors shook her body. Maybe we were both shaking.

Lisa

Pop and Elsie joined us at the police station where Jake and I had to give our statements. My hands still shook, even after two hours.

When Jake mentioned the FBI, I fumbled through my purse, searching for Agent Farrow's card. I finally found it, slightly wrinkled, and handed it to the detective.

After we were released, Allison headed home in her car.

Elsie kept insisting we stop at the hospital. She rubbed my back. "Jake was bitten, and you have an ugly gash on your arm. You could have internal injuries as well."

I started laughing and couldn't stop. The way she'd said *Jake was bitten* struck me funny. I'm not sure why. It wasn't at all humorous.

"See there," Elsie said. "You're in shock. Pop, make them go to the emergency room."

Pop looked at Jake. "It probably wouldn't hurt. That guy might have rabies."

Jake guffawed.

We all laughed except Elsie, who stood with her arms crossed at her waist, brow furrowed.

Pop stepped to a nearby pay phone and called their family doctor. Then he drove us over to Dr. Hill's office.

Dr. Hill's nurse escorted Jake and me to separate exam rooms. After a thorough examination, I was pronounced well except for a few bruises.

"Take it easy for a couple of days," Dr. Hill told me.

Thank goodness, neither of us needed stitches. Jake was given an antibiotic ointment and told to keep his wound clean and dry.

Jake and I sat in Pop's back seat on the way home. Pop and Elsie kept up a running conversation in the front, talking about crop futures and cattle prices. The silence next to me was deafening. Somehow, I knew Jake wasn't hearing their conversation.

I touched his hand. "Was that the guy?"

His eyes met mine. He gave a slight nod but didn't speak.

If we had been alone, I would have pressed for more information. Did this mean I was free now? The last felon had been apprehended. A tremor shook me.

Jake took my hand. "Are you okay?"

Tears threatened. I blinked them back and nodded. "I will be."

I had discovered another downside to having a real family. The pain of parting.

Pop pulled my car into the front drive as I stepped onto the porch with my suitcase. When he got out, I noticed something in the backseat.

He removed his cap and scratched his head. "That's Mama's doing. Allison's, too."

I looked past him to an overstuffed laundry basket, tied up with a big, red bow, behind the driver's seat. A lump clogged my throat. I had hoped to get through this without tears, but they were making it really hard.

The front door swung open, and Elsie stepped out. "That's a dorm basket, hon. Everything you need for your room back at school."

Allison walked toward me with a wide smile on her face. "I didn't tell Mama about the break-in. Ben did." She held her hands out and shrugged. "So, Mama and I went shopping."

"You didn't have to do that."

Elsie put her arm around me. "I know but it sure was fun."

I hadn't noticed Pop leaving until he came back out with Jake. I stepped forward to open the trunk.

Pop cackled. "I'll never get used to seeing that. Trunk in the front. Not much of one, though."

I pointed to the luggage rack. "Which is why I have that."

Elsie took my hand. "All packed up and ready to go, aren't you? We sure are going to miss you, sugar." She hugged me and planted a kiss on my cheek. "Now, you call collect when you get there. Let us know you're all right, you hear?"

"I will." I drew back and smiled into her eyes.

Allison hugged me next. "I'm going to miss you, too. This time, write me back, okay?"

I laughed, especially when I noticed the look on Jake's face. I suppose no one had told him about the letters. "I'll make sure to write as often as I can."

Pop was next. He laid his hand on my shoulder and whispered in my ear, "When God places someone in your path, girl, don't avoid that person. Give God time to work things out."

I figured he meant Jake, so I nodded, but maybe I

needed to give his advice some thought.

Everyone stopped talking when a dark blue car turned the corner onto Sundrop Lane and pulled into the drive.

Jake looked back at me. "Looks like Farrow found us."

I stepped beside Jake and watched as Agent Farrow got out of the passenger door of the sedan and walked toward us.

Agent Evers rolled down the window and nodded a greeting.

Jake moved forward. "Farrow?"

Farrow looked past him to nod at me, Pop, Elsie, and Allison. "Morning, Miss Oliver. Everyone." He squared off with Jake. "I thought I told you not to engage."

For a moment, I thought he was serious. Then he grinned. I was pretty sure I'd never seen him smile.

Jake's shoulders slumped a little. "I wasn't going to let him have her." He glanced at me and winked.

Something fluttered in my stomach. My cheeks warmed.

Ever the good hostess, Elsie offered coffee.

Farrow signaled Agent Evers. "I won't turn that down. I need to speak to all of you, anyway."

Agent Evers joined us as we all headed inside. Seated around the living room, Agent Farrow made small talk with Jake and Pop until Elsie and Allison returned with coffee for everyone.

Allison sat beside me on the sofa.

My plans for an early start thwarted, I glanced at the clock on the mantel and then back at Farrow. How long would he stay?

After stirring an inordinate amount of sugar into his coffee, he faced Pop. "First of all, I want to assure you and your family that we have this situation under control."

Pop frowned. "Just what is the situation, Agent Farrow?"

After a quick look at Jake, Farrow answered. "We have now apprehended the second suspect alleged to be involved in the deaths of Mr. and Mrs. Oliver."

My back went rigid. I needed answers. "But why did they come after me? I wasn't even there when the accident occurred."

Farrow looked at me as though he'd forgotten I was in the room. "At this time, I'm not free to comment, Miss Oliver. I can assure you, as soon as we know the facts, I will pass them along."

My eyes sought Jake's. He was focused on Farrow. Jake set his cup down. "So, why are you here?"

Farrow tilted his head sideways. "Agent Evers and I

are here to escort you and Miss Oliver back to Kentucky."

My jaw dropped. "Escort? Why?"

Allison laid her hand on mine.

Farrow turned to me. "We cannot allow the two of you to drive that distance unaccompanied."

I looked at Jake. We were still in danger.

Farrow sipped his coffee before looking at me. "I suggest you leave your car here, with your friends. Agent Evers and I will deliver you to your dorm."

I shook my head. "No. No, you can't. I won't have a vehicle."

Jake leaned toward me. "You won't really need one, Lisa."

My gaze flitted from one to another of my friends. Would no one take my side?

Elsie came to stand behind me. Her hands on my shoulders reassured me. "They're just trying to protect you, Lisa. It's for the best."

Farrow set his cup on the tray. "It was strongly recommended that you be moved into protective custody until after the trial, Miss Oliver. I was made aware of your desire to continue your schooling, so I asked for a special provision. At present, we'll be able to ensure your safety once you're on campus. If all goes well, you should be able to return for your car at Christmas."

If all goes well. Winter break was three months away.

Allison gave my hand a squeeze. "You were planning to come home for Christmas anyway."

I looked into her eyes. She was so certain. Why couldn't I feel that?

Jake's voice broke into my little pity party. "What's this 'special provision' you mentioned?"

Farrow sat forward. "That's something we can discuss on the road." He stood. "Mr. and Mrs. Pearl, thank you for your hospitality."

Numb inside, I remained in place, even when everyone else stood to go. For a few short hours, I had dared to hope for a normal life. Once again, it had been torn from my grasp.

CHAPTER FORTY-TWO

Lisa

"My purse?" I glared at Agent Farrow. I was not giving him my purse.

He sat sideways in the passenger seat, his eyes on me. He shook his head and sighed. "Just go through it, pull out anything that identifies you."

I frowned.

Jake laid his hand on my forearm. "It's for your protection, Lisa."

I pressed my hands against my abdomen. *Deep breath. Slow exhale. Don't look at Farrow.*

This was his fault. Had he leaked our whereabouts to that guy, Petrov? Put us in harm's way, as he'd done with Jake a couple of weeks ago? I wanted to spew my anger at him. Let him know what I thought. Instead, I did as I was told. Like a good little girl. My fingers shook as I sifted through the contents of my purse. I removed all my I.D. cards. My drivers' license. Anything with my name on it.

Jake took them from me and held them until I had finished. Then he passed them to Farrow, who tucked them into his breast pocket.

My hands in my lap, I stared out the window.

Jake rubbed my arm. "I'm sorry, Lisa."

I faced him.

A small smile quirked his lips. Probably an attempt at comfort. Reassurance.

If we were alone, I could lean against him and allow him to comfort me. An ache pushed through my selfish anxiety. He had to be hurting, too. I held his gaze until Farrow spoke again.

"From this point on, you'll be known as Renee Roberts." He passed me a couple of cards. "This is all you will need."

I forced myself to look at the I.D. cards, replacements for everything except my license. My heart thudded against my chest as I read the name. At least it would be easy to remember. My middle name and Mom's first name, sort of. Roberts instead of Roberta.

I raised my eyes to Agent Farrow. "What about my friends? They'll still call me Lisa."

"That won't be a concern. We've moved you to a safer building. You'll have a new roommate."

"Not Shelby?"

"Your former roommate transferred to the University of Louisville School of Psychology."

I sat back as Farrow continued. Too many changes. I struggled to take it in.

"Your new roommate's name is Linda Montgomery. She's an undercover police officer. She'll be your shadow."

My shadow. I wrapped my arms around myself and gave in to misery as the men continued to talk.

The drone of their voices blended with the roar of the tires. I closed my eyes and pretended to sleep.

Linda Montgomery didn't look like a police officer. She didn't seem old enough. She had honey blonde hair, green eyes, and a liberal sprinkling of freckles across her nose. Her smile set me at ease as she pitched in to help move me into the dorm.

She stayed in the room as I walked back out with Jake.

I knew it was time, but I wasn't ready to say goodbye.

Evers and Farrow leaned against the car, taking a smoke break.

Jake took my hands in his and gazed into my eyes. "I'm going to miss you, kid."

I took a breath and eased it out, gathering courage. "Jake, I want you to drop the story."

He drew back. "What?"

I shook my head. "It's too dangerous. If something happens to you—" my voice broke.

He pulled me forward and wrapped his arms around me. I relaxed against him. My head rested against his chest as I listened to his heartbeat. It felt right. Perfect.

When I drew back, he looked into my eyes.

Before he could speak, I pressed forward. "I'm serious. You said it was my decision. Please stop, Jake. Let it go."

If I asked for a promise, would he give it? Could he?

Farrow's voice interrupted. "If you two lovebirds are finished, we need to get back on the road."

Jake pressed a kiss against my brow. "I'll see you at Christmas."

I stepped back and spoke through trembling lips. "Christmas."

"I'll write. I'll send postcards."

I shook my head. "Not if it compromises your safety."

He thought for a moment. "What was your favorite television character?"

"We didn't always have a TV."

His shoulders rose and fell. "I'll come up with something, then. We'll figure it out." He drew my hand to his lips, kissed it, and smiled.

"When we did have a television, Mom loved to watch Bonanza. She liked Little Joe."

"Little Joe. Okay." He let go of my hand.

"Just walk away, Renee," Farrow said. "Come on, Bradley."

Jake groaned. "Is he actually making a joke right now with that old song?"

Though I longed to return to his embrace and stay there, I stepped back. "Take care of yourself, Benjamin Bradley."

With two thumbs up, he turned his back on me and strode toward the car.

I was going to miss him.

Acknowledgements

Writing is a solitary pursuit but once the story is written, it takes a team of book elves to work out the kinks. I am blessed with three such elves. Actually, they are the talented writers on my critique loop. Now, there are only two because one graduated to Heaven this past year. Thank you, Gail Johnson and Kristy Horine.

Many, many, thanks, Nike Navor Chillemi. I was blessed to call you a friend. I miss you and your thriller/detective novels. Most of all, I miss our long email convos and your snarky humor. We'll see you again one day.

Even when you think your work is complete and oh, so perfect, it is shipped off to the editors who rip it to shreds, all the while assuring you the story is a good one— you just have to find it. This has never been truer for me than with this latest work. I so appreciate the patience of my editors. Thanks for believing a story was hidden beneath all that, Marji Laine Clubine and Brittany Deane.

Special thanks as always to my publisher, Marji Laine Clubine for taking a chance on me and believing I could write a suspense novel.

My life growing up inspired much of this story. Well,

not the darker side of it, but the meandering all over the country part. I have my wonderful parents to thank for that. They inspired me to dream and believe I could do anything I set my mind to. Our travels taught me resiliency and acceptance. An adventure lies just around that next bend. Thanks Mom, and Dad (in Heaven). All my love, always.

Thanks to the love of my life, my husband, Bob, who tolerates my hibernating in our home for hours and days on end, writing, writing. He supports me (literally), encourages me, and gives me comfy robes and house slippers so I don't freeze at my desk. He inspires much of the humor in my stories, especially the male characters.

To all my readers who never hesitate to ask when my next book is coming out and why is it taking so long, thanks for keeping the fire lit beneath me. Without you, I may have quit this stuff long ago.

Faith in God and trust in Christ keeps me moving forward through all the calamities of life. Great is His Faithfulness!

About the Author

 Betty Thomason Owens was born in an Army hospital in the Pacific Northwest but grew up in California, Tennessee, and Kentucky. An avid reader and storyteller from a young age, she didn't begin a writing career until her late thirties. In 2011, she attended a local writers conference where she was encouraged to continue writing. After self-publishing a couple of fantasy novels, she received a contract for her first historical romance series. Her stories often feature strong women dealing with difficult life situations.

Now a multi-published writer of historical romance, suspense, and fantasy fiction, she and her husband reside in Kentucky. They have three grown sons and seven grandchildren. You can learn more about her at BettyThomasonOwens.com. Connect with her on Facebook, Twitter, Pinterest, and Instagram.

Mystery & Suspense
from Pursued Books

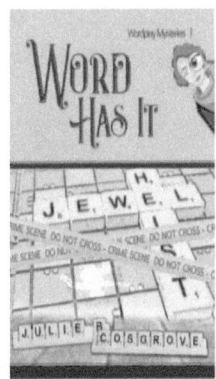

Thank you
for reading our books!

Look for other books
published by

P

Pursued Books
an imprint of

W

Write Integrity Press
www.WriteIntegrity.com